Wisler
My Brother, the Wind

My Brother, the Wind

My Brother, the Wind

G. CLIFTON WISLER

DOUBLEDAY & COMPANY, INC.

GARDEN CITY, NEW YORK

1979

ISBN: 0-385-14822-4
Library of Congress Catalog Card Number: 78-14690

Library of Congress Cataloging in Publication Data

Wisler, G Clifton.
  My brother, the wind.

  I. Title.
PZ4.W8246My [PS3573.I877]   813'.5'4

For my grandparents,
who epitomize the best
of the American West

Prologue

In the spring of 1877, a group of traders camping along the Yellowstone River in northern Wyoming reported a strange sight. A lone rider of slight build appeared, dressed in deerskin clothes and a huge bearskin coat. He rode a small Indian pony into their midst, leading behind him three mules laden with pelts and buffalo hides.

The traders, who claimed to know all of the trappers of the upper Yellowstone, did not recognize this newcomer. They were further amazed to detect on his person a war shirt with Shoshoni markings, a necklace of bear claws, a Cheyenne war bracelet, a Crow hunting knife and a Sioux war lance. Knowing these tribes to be notorious enemies, they first discounted the newcomer as a green easterner who had gone souvenir hunting at an army post.

Later, they thought he might be a former cavalryman. But as he continued to approach, their eyes told them this was not the case.

The rider led his horses to their campfire and dismounted. When his feet at last touched the ground, the traders saw that their visitor stood barely five feet six inches tall. Despite the heavy bearskin coat, it was clear that his thin shoulders and wiry frame belonged to a boy.

Where did he come from? Who was he? What was he doing in the Yellowstone Valley? The traders didn't ask. It was common among the semiwild men of the mountains to have secrets themselves, and it was not their way to pry into the background of another.

After trading gold for the beautiful pelts the boy had brought down from the mountains, they gathered around the campfire to exchange tales. The boy sat stone-faced, silent. The next morning they found that he had disappeared without a trace.

When the traders spread the story in the small towns that were sprouting up along the railroad, they met with a similar tale.

A boy, clothed in deerskin with a bearskin coat, had sold three mules and several buffalo hides to another trader. When the trader had asked the boy about the army bounty on buffalo hides, the boy's eyes had burned with anger. After their bargain was made, the boy had his flowing blond hair trimmed, traded horses, and then set out with a small wagon train headed for Oregon.

Many stories sprang up to explain the young man. He had been raised by Indians and finally escaped. He was the son of a mountain man and had decided to return to civilization.

The truth was only known to a few soldiers, some buffalo hunters, an old Crow warrior, the boy's family and the boy himself. And the spirits of the mountains, if there are such things.

I

There is a legend among the Crow people that on the day of a man's birth, a new star appears in the heavens. The fate of star and man is linked, and the one cannot outshine or outlast the other. A man is born to his life, so says the legend, and it is his lot to follow his star.

I do not know if the legend is true. I've known men who believed in spirits and legends, but who's to say if they are so? I myself have seen things that should not be, but there is something in the mountains that clouds a man's eyes.

For my part, I was not born to the mountains.

My life began in the winter of 1861. War clouds had gathered over the land, and the sounds of cannons and muskets echoed through the quiet Ohio River Valley to which I was born. It was a harsh time. The men were mustered in army camps to the south. Snows blew across the land, freezing stock. Woodpiles shrank, and women and children huddled together against the cold, praying that their husbands and brothers and fathers would be home for Christmas. None of them were.

I came into the world that hard October, born in the midst of the winter's first blizzard. It was not a choice time to be born, but one does not choose the time of his arrival on this earth. I was told my grandparents feared for the life of my mother. She was a frail woman, and she'd already borne eight children, six of them still living. Aunt Agnes and my father had hoped I would not come into the world at the cost of my mother's life.

Near midnight on the sixteenth my voice finally greeted the world with a terrible whine. All around were delighted. My mother suffered in bed for the rest of the month, but by November she was well again.

My brother Matthew told me Father was pleased. He'd gotten permission from his general to stay home until winter passed. Matthew remembered the man held me often in the evenings. When the snows melted, my father mounted his horse, flashed his sabre, and promised to send Mother some new china when the army marched into New Orleans.

Father was Captain John Timothy Welles, captain of the Fifth Ohio Cavalry. I still have a photograph Mother gave me of him in his proud uniform. He rode away that cruel afternoon in January, never to return. He fell to Confederate musket fire at Shiloh that April.

My family endured the war years better than most. There were six boys among us, and Joseph, Thomas and Isaac were all of an age to help with the farm. We made our harvest every year, and Mother managed the accounts with great skill and courage.

Joseph took a wife in the winter of 1864. Her name was Helen Glebov. She was always a favorite of mine since she was forever making a fuss over me. They were both but seventeen, and it was asked by some of the neighbors if, with the war raging and all, Joseph wasn't perhaps taking a young widow. But they were truly in love. I learned later that they raised nine children to adulthood.

The second eldest was my sister Martha. She was the only girl that had lived through childhood, and she was a bad lot. She kicked the younger boys, especially me, without mercy. She turned sixteen the winter of 1864.

Thomas and Isaac came next. They were fifteen and fourteen, and both were adventurers. They would tell me stories of kings and palaces and how one day they would go off to California and strike it rich.

Matthew was nine. He could already read and write, though, and Mother often sought his help with the accounts.

Matthew missed Father more than the rest. It was from Matthew that I learned of the man, and I suppose I was closer to him than the others as a result.

Between Matthew and myself came my brother Robert. Robert was six, and he was Mother's favorite, next to me. Robert could already read a little. Mother read beautifully, and she was determined that her younger children would learn at an early age the skills of reading and writing.

The winter of 1864 was a cold one, even for the war years. There was never enough wood in the fireplace to keep us warm. Matthew, Robert and I tried to keep warm under three old blankets. We would go to sleep as soon as the fire died out, hoping the warmth would last awhile.

Most of the time it didn't, and we would shiver through the night side by side. Aunt Agnes, who was really my mother's aunt, swore you couldn't have slipped a feather between us. I thought during that winter that the sun would never come up again.

It almost didn't for me. In late December I was taken with a fever. I couldn't even keep soup down, and Helen swore she'd skin Robert alive if I died.

Robert had pushed me into a snow bank before it happened, but Mother said it was just the cold and the way children are that brought the fever. Robert watched over me many nights, though, and I often heard his prayers.

The worst of the fever hit near Christmas. A doctor from the next township arrived and pronounced that I would die. I don't remember any of it. Aunt Agnes told me she whipped Thomas and Isaac for betting on which day I'd die. Helen would bathe me in her tears.

Aunt Agnes said that after I was almost taken one night, Mother moved me to her bed. She'd fret and worry over me all night. One night, Aunt Agnes told me, Mother was bent over the bed in prayer.

"God, take me and not little Timothy," she pleaded.

God answered her and spared me. But he drove a hard bargain. In January my brothers and I buried her in a simple grave marked by a plain wooden cross. That same month, we buried Grandpa and Grandma Welles beside her.

I cried every night that January. I kept dreaming that I'd forget what she looked like. I had a picture of Father, but I only had my memory of Mother. Then one night Martha took my little hand and led me to a big trunk in the kitchen.

It was Father's army trunk. General Grant had sent it home after Shiloh. His uniform was in there, sword and all. There was a giant Colt revolver, too, and some other clothes. There was also a silver locket with Mother's picture.

The face was younger than the one I'd known, but the eyes were the same. I clutched it to my chest and started crying all over again.

"You're to stop that crying, Timothy," Martha scolded me. "You may have the locket if you promise to weep no more for her. She has gone to heaven and greater glory than you will. You bear your father's name. Show courage!"

Martha took me up in her lap and stroked my hair back out of my eyes. She held me until I fell asleep, singing softly to me as my mother had done. It was the only time Martha ever showed me that she loved me. After that, I always knew it, even when she chased me around the farm with a hoe.

As I grew into a young lad, I remained thin and frail, like my mother. Each winter my brothers feared the first frost would take me. But I managed to hold on.

The war clouds passed, and the years rolled on. Martha married a young army captain, Ronald Pierson, and went off to the Oregon Territory in 1866.

Martha wrote letters telling of their difficult passage. There were Indians, blizzards, floods, deserts. But they survived it all, and by 1869 they had a fine little farm in the Willamette Valley. Martha was expecting her first child in the spring, and her letters beckoned us to join them.

Joseph and Helen had three children by then. Thomas and Isaac were restless, and it was clear the farm would not support two more families. They were anxious to find California and their dreams of panning for gold and striking it rich.

On Christmas Eve, 1869, we decided the farm would

pass to Joseph and Helen. Aunt Agnes, who was approaching her eightieth year, would stay and help with the children. Thomas and Isaac would be given money for stock and supplies for a trip to Oregon, where they could join Martha or go south to California.

Matthew and Robert, who were too young to set out on their own, decided to stay in Ohio. Matthew wanted to be a lawyer, and both of them were needed on the farm. That left me.

Helen wanted me to stay. I was only eight, just four years older than her eldest son, James. But there was a spirit of adventure in me, and I wanted to see the Rocky Mountains and the Willamette Valley. I chose to go with Thomas and Isaac.

Thomas and Isaac were not exactly overjoyed about this. Their great adventure would be limited considerably by my presence. But Joseph insisted I had as much right to the wagon and stock as they did, so it was decided I would cross the mountains.

When the snows melted and the wagon was ready, Thomas and Isaac checked the harness and the provisions. I sneaked away and made my way to the little graveyard and sat down.

"Mother, I'm leaving for Oregon," I told her. "I can read and write, and I'm growing stronger. The frosts don't frighten me, nor do the Indians and the deserts. I will be clean in body and spirit. Good-bye."

I ran to catch up with Thomas and Isaac. Jumping onto the back of the wagon, I waved a tearful good-bye to the rest of my family. I figured I'd never see any of them again.

I took with me on my great journey westward the clothes I wore plus three cotton shirts, two pairs of overalls, and an extra pair of boots I'd inherited from Matthew and Robert. There was also a box of books Matthew had insisted I take. Lastly, I had Father's portrait, the locket of Mother, and the huge army Colt revolver my father had carried at Shiloh.

As the wagon rambled toward Cincinnati, I fingered the bulletless gun and tried not to cry. There were many miles ahead of us, and countless hazards and hardships.

II

Cincinnati in 1870 was a bustling town. I'd never seen so many people at one time, all hurrying around in different directions. Thomas drove the wagon straight to the waterfront, so I only had a chance to observe from the rear of the wagon. But a grander sight than that, I'd never seen.

Thomas stopped the wagon at a wharf and went over to some boatmen. Isaac followed him, but I knew my place was to stay with the wagon. My brothers were talking loudly with the boatmen. One of the boatmen pointed to our wagon and shook his head. Another broke out laughing.

Isaac stomped his foot hard and yelled something. Thomas, though, quieted him and talked to the big man in the center. The big man pointed again to our wagon and laughed. Finally, Thomas shook his head and walked away, followed by Isaac.

"What'd they say?" I asked when they returned.

"They say we can't take the wagon to Independence," said Isaac. "He said we might be able to get her to St. Louis on a boat, but we'd never get to Independence in time to make the spring train going overland from there.

He said we should sell the wagon and go by boat to St. Louis, then catch a ride on the railroad to Independence."

"Can we get a wagon in Independence?" I asked.

"Look, little brother," Thomas said, patting me on the shoulder. "Don't you worry. We're going across the mountains."

We drove the wagon up and down the wharf trying to find a boat to take the wagon. None of them would do it for less than a fortune. Finally, Thomas made a deal to sell the wagon and book passage on a big riverboat to Cairo.

I hated leaving the wagon behind. It was just another part of home we parted with. But Cincinnati was a busy freight center, and Thomas was able to get a good price for the wagon and horses.

I forced myself to smile as we carried our boxes and trunks on board the riverboat. We had to share a little cabin that was sometimes used to haul stock, but I was a farm boy, and I was used to the feel of straw and the smell of cattle.

There were a lot of people on the boat headed for Oregon or California. Big families, discouraged soldiers, fortune hunters, adventurers, trappers and even newlyweds. There was one family, the Hudsons, who especially befriended us.

Mrs. Hudson was a big jolly kind of a woman. She always seemed to have a little extra candy or bread for me. She told Thomas and Isaac stories of her brother in San Francisco.

Mr. Hudson was a short, stocky man. He was a blacksmith. He'd served in the infantry in Tennessee, but he told me he wasn't at Shiloh. He could pick me up with either hand, but there was a gentleness to him, too.

Best of all, they had a son. His name was Jerome, and he was fourteen. He reminded me a lot of my brother Matthew. Jerome and I ran wild on the riverboat. We climbed everything, poked our heads where they had no business being, and were declared universal nuisances. The cook swore if he caught us in another pie, he'd pickle our heads for the captain's table.

The captain just laughed. He'd been a gunboat captain during the war, and he marveled at my big Colt revolver. He offered to buy it, but I refused. It was my father's, I had explained. He'd understood.

The first mate, Mr. Gundarson, showed us all over the ship. Whenever he could find time, he'd tell us stories about Mike Fink and Davy Crockett and the taming of the Mississippi. Jerome and I would sit speechless and listen to him for hours.

When the ship docked at Cairo, I hated to get off. My only consolation was that Jerome and his family were also going West. They took the same boat we did to St. Louis.

I'd heard stories all my life about the Mississippi. At Cairo, the Mississippi and the Ohio merge, and it was one of the grandest sights I'd ever seen. The two great rivers flow together to make one enormous sea of water. Where they fork, the town of Cairo sprang up to take advantage of the commerce flowing from three directions.

We stayed overnight in Cairo. Jerome and I slept in a stable. Mr. and Mrs. Hudson got a hotel room. Thomas and Isaac wanted some adventure, so they headed for a bawdy house down by the river. All the way to St. Louis, I heard them telling each other stories. They'd talk just loud enough that I could suspect what they were saying, but too softly for me to get any of the details.

The trip up the Mississippi was a short one. It was only about 150 miles upriver to St. Louis, less than half what we'd traveled down the Ohio. Thomas and Isaac spent most of their time playing cards and talking to young ladies. I spent most of mine with Jerome, talking about what the trip West would be like.

We met Mr. Brannigan on the boat. He was a real-life mountain man. He'd made the crossing a dozen times, and he showed us the knife with which he'd killed three Flathead Indians.

I was filled with the spirit of adventure by this man. He'd hunted buffalo, fought Indians, killed bears and climbed mountains. He told us he came East every so often to see his family. It surprised me that such a man would come back East at all with such adventure waiting for him in the mountains.

One day Jerome and I learned from one of the first-class stewards that Mr. Brannigan was nothing but a liar. He'd never been west of St. Louis. I was really mad, but Jerome told me to forget it.

"They were good stories, weren't they?" he asked me. "What difference does it make if they were all made up?"

I wasn't quite so easy to fool from then on. As I learned later, the real mountain men very rarely came out of the mountains. And they almost never spoke to anyone.

In St. Louis, we got on a train. Jerome and his family rode up front in a passenger car. Thomas had heard stories about the prices of things in Independence, and he was worried we might not have enough money for everything we needed, so we rode in a freight car. It was a long trip, mainly because the train stopped so often. But I was getting used to the feel of straw and the smell of stock, and I was eager to start the trail West.

We mostly ate dried beef and bread on the train, so I was pretty thin when we reached Independence. Thomas took us to a big tent that served as a restaurant, and we ate a big steak, heaps of potatoes and all kinds of vegetables. I thought I could eat forever, but I finally got my fill. Thomas turned green when he paid the man for the food. It was as much as we paid for our passage down the Ohio.

We slept in a tent made from canvas Isaac had salvaged from the wagon we'd sold in Cincinnati. It rained all night, but not having to share my bed with a cow, I slept like a log.

The next morning we got up early and set out to find a wagon. We stumbled onto the Hudsons, and the six of us walked up Main Street trying to find the right wagon for the right price.

We were amazed to find that there were several good wagons available. Even more amazing, they were cheap. We bought a wagon, a team of oxen, a horse, and all our supplies for less than we'd sold the wagon for at Cincinnati. Thomas and I were excited, but Mr. Hudson was worried. His concern soon spread to Isaac, who decided to check it out.

"Why were we able to get such a good deal on our wagons?" Isaac asked an old, worn-looking man in front of a saloon.

"Well," the old man said, scratching his chin. "Most folks don't buy their wagons until they're ready to start the trail."

"We're ready," said Isaac.

"Why, it's already June," the man said. "Won't be another train for a year. Trains that start in June ends up snowbound."

We exchanged looks of disgust.

"Isn't there anyway to get West now?" asked Thomas.

"Sure," the man smiled. "Just follow the sun. Always sets in the west. But ain't many make it past Fort Laramie. Injuns get 'em."

We made camp outside of town that night. We were all discouraged. We knew that we couldn't wait until next year. Our stock would die. Our money would be gone. We'd either have to go on or go back.

"Well, boys," said Mr. Hudson. "I'm for going on. I haven't got anything behind me. But you boys'd be better off going home to your brother."

"Oh, no," said Thomas. "Not me. Isaac and I've dreamed of going West since we were five. If there's not another train until next year, then we'll just make it on our own. There are four of us, counting Jerome, that can shoot. If we don't run into a tribe of Indians, we should make it."

Isaac nodded his head, but Mrs. Hudson spoke up.

"And what about Timothy?" she asked.

"We'll send him back to Ohio," Thomas said.

"Oh, no you won't," I objected. "I'm old enough. I'll get some bullets for my gun and show them Indians a thing or two."

Thomas laughed, but I ran over to him.

"I'm going," I insisted.

"Yes," said Thomas. "You are. You're going back to Ohio."

We spent the next two days getting ready and resting

the stock. Then we got lucky and met Bear Claw Sullivan.

Bear Claw was a frontier scout. He was headed for Ft. Riley, just south of the main route of the Oregon Trail. Bear Claw didn't talk much, so it was a pure accident that I ran across him. I was waiting for Thomas and Isaac outside a saloon when I saw him.

"Are you really a mountain man?" I asked, running over to him.

"Nope," he mumbled, biting into a slug of tobacco.

"You been West?" I asked.

"Been everywhere," he answered.

"To Ft. Laramie?"

"Been to the top of the mountain and the other side of the moon," he said. "Seen the end of the rainbow and the bottom of the earth."

I didn't understand.

"Couldn't you take me to Ft. Laramie?" I asked.

"Could," he said, laughing. "Won't."

"Why not?" I asked.

"You ask too many fool questions, boy," he said. "It's 'nough to know I won't."

I turned my head away from him and dropped my head into my hands. I was beginning to think I wouldn't make it West after all.

"You could make it to Ft. Laramie, though," he said, sitting beside me.

"How?" I asked.

"I go to Ft. Riley tomorrow. You follow me there. I ride hard and fast, but you keep up, I'll get you there."

"And the Indians?"

"Mostly Kiowa. Custer's been fightin' them. Mostly,

they're tired. No Indian trouble 'tween here and Ft. Riley."

"And past there?"

"Just Cheyenne and Sioux," he said, laughing. "Them and Black Feet. Just the meanest devils in the West. They'd as soon slit your throat or the rest of you as smile."

"Then how're we going to get there?" I asked.

"Might be some cavalry going that way. Heard rumors 'bout it. They might take you along."

I hurried to tell Thomas and Isaac and the Hudsons. Thomas came flying out of the saloon.

"Mr. Sullivan," my brother said, "how're we to thank you?"

"Not me. I like kids with spunk." Bear Claw smiled at me. "I was with Fitzpatrick going to California in '43. Just about his age," he added, pointing to me. "They say Broken Hand Fitzpatrick was the meanest man that ever lived. They was right until I came along. Keep up with me or I'll leave you behind. You get left, just follow the wagon ruts."

"Thanks," Thomas said.

"You travel with me, you might even catch the last train up in Wyoming. That way you could finish your crossing with them."

It all sounded terrific to us. Bear Claw got us going hard right off. Jerome and I walked, Thomas rode, Isaac and the Hudsons drove. We stopped only for water, following the path cut in the prairie by the thousands of wagons that had gone before us.

Most of the trip followed the trail, but when it swung north away from the Republican River, Bear Claw led us on beside the river.

"There's plenty of water this way," he informed us, "and if you lose me, you can follow the river right into Ft. Riley."

We traveled about fifteen miles a day, stopping only when there was no light remaining. I was worn out and fell asleep after dinner. Mrs. Hudson cooked for everyone, and I began to suspect Bear Claw wouldn't leave us behind after all. He might not care about the rest of us, but he'd greatly regret leaving Mrs. Hudson's cooking behind.

After the first few days, I walked half of the time, slept in the wagon the other half. It was Bear Claw's idea, and Thomas went along with it. Even so, I was worn out after the day and had no energy left for games or songs or anything.

Bear Claw would get out his Tennessee harmonica and sing mournful trail songs at night. They usually put me to sleep, but his deep, sorrowful voice singing "Shenandoah" made me cry.

"How old are you?" I asked him one night.

"What year is this?" he asked in turn.

"Eighteen-seventy," I told him.

"Then I'm thirty-six years old," he said. "Myself, I've no use for times and years."

"Do you have any children?" I asked him.

"Got a boy and two girls at Ft. Riley," he said.

"And a wife?" I asked.

"Squaw," he said. "Crow. Ugly old sow, but she can do things with corn meal no white woman could. 'Sides, she suits me. She mends, sews, and don't make no fuss over me."

"Your children are half Indian?"

"You got somethin' to say, say it!" he growled.

I backed away from him. I was surprised to see him angry.

"I was just wondering what they looked like," I explained.

Bear Claw laughed heartily.

"Shoulda known," he said. "Somes got opinions it ain't right for a white man to take a squaw. Me, I's seen all kinds of men. I know they're all the same in most ways. Indian's brave, proud, strong."

"Are they good?" I asked.

"Most of 'em. Take my boy. He can outride anyone at the fort. He's handsome. They says Crow is the most handsome of all Indians."

"Are the girls pretty?" I asked.

"A little young, aren't you?" he asked, smiling.

"I was just wondering," I said.

"The boy's twelve. Girls are pretty little things of four and six. I's hoping they won't take after their father or their mother."

We sat together silently for a while. Then he began singing "Shenandoah," and I thought about my mother. When he finished, I turned to him.

"Do you ever think of home?" I asked.

"Got no home," he said, frowning.

"What about Tennessee?" I asked him.

"Left her when I was seven. My ma and pa died on the trail. Got a sister in San Francisco, a brother in Sacramento. My only home is a saddle."

"I'm sorry," I said. "I think a man needs a home."

"What for?" he asked me.

"I'm not sure," I said. "Maybe to sing about. Maybe to miss when he's lonely."

"Maybe," he said, picking up the harmonica. "Maybe."

I left him playing some of his old trail songs. Then I said good night to everyone and went to bed.

I lost track of the number of days we were on the trail to Ft. Riley. As the days rolled by, I grew stronger. By the time we got to the fort, I was able to walk most of the day without tiring.

The fort wasn't at all what I expected. I thought it would be a stockade down by the river. There were, instead, strong walls with cannons mounted. The buildings were mostly stone. As Bear Claw led us inside the walls, I saw soldiers drilling on the parade ground. They were mostly cavalry, and I trotted over to an old sergeant while Thomas accompanied Bear Claw to the headquarters building.

"Hello," I said to the big burly man. "Are you a cavalry man?"

"You bet," he said. "Company C, Seventh Cavalry."

"My father rode with the Fifth Ohio Cavalry at Shiloh," I said. "This is his gun," I added, pulling out the massive Colt and pointing it at him.

"Watch it, boy," the sergeant yelled, diving to the ground. "Put that cannon away!"

I heard a big laugh behind me. Turning, I saw a tall man dressed in buckskin.

"I led Ohio cavalry at Gettysburg and Cold Harbor," the man said. "Was your father there?"

"No," I sighed. "He died at Shiloh."

The man reached over and put his hand on my shoulder.

"That's a shame," he said. "Many of the best men fell in battle. Tell me about him."

I sat down on the wooden porch of the barracks and told him about my father.

"I don't really remember him," I said. "I was just a baby."

He sat down beside me and turned my head toward him.

"Where you headed?" he asked me.

"Ft. Laramie," I said. "Bear Claw told us he thought we might be able to catch a wagon train there."

"Laramie's full of Cheyenne and Sioux," he told me. "We're sending a detachment up there soon to beef up the fort. The whole area's swarming with Indians. You'd be better off to head south. Maybe you'd like to try Colorado or the Southwest."

"My sister's waitin' in Oregon," I explained.

"Your ma might like to keep her hair."

"My mother's dead," I said, wiping a tear away. "We left her in Ohio."

"Then maybe I'd better have a talk with the general about you. You have a name?"

"Timothy Tobias Welles," I told him.

"Mine's Custer," the man said. "I'm a colonel, Seventh U. S. Cavalry. Was a general in the war, but I got myself in a bit of trouble. On my way back to Ft. Hays now."

"My father knew a general," I said. "General Grant. He's President now."

"I know," the man said. "He's the reason I'm a colonel," he explained, grinding his teeth against each other. "Timothy, I'd like you and your party to be my guests for dinner. I'll send a man."

"Thanks," I told him.

When I rejoined my family, I ran to Thomas.

"Guess what," I said. "We're going to have dinner with a colonel."

"Sure," he said, frowning. "Only problem is we won't be here. The general told us he couldn't be responsible for us making a crossing to Ft. Laramie. He said the Sioux and the Cheyenne are all stirred up. We're going anyway."

"Maybe Colonel Custer can help us," I said.

"Who?" asked Mr. Hudson. "Did you say Custer?"

"Yes," I told them. "He asked us to dinner. I showed him Father's gun."

"That may be our way out," Mr. Hudson said. "Custer's sending some men up to Ft. Laramie. He's fought the Kiowa and the Shawnees. They won't mess with the army. The Sioux won't want to tangle with the cavalry, either."

"Might be," Thomas said, smiling and patting me on the back. "Now tell us all about your meeting with General Custer."

"He's a colonel," I said.

"That's all political," Thomas said. "He's still a mighty big man hereabouts."

That night we ate dinner with the "general." He had discarded his buckskins and was wearing a full-dress uniform. His wife was there, too. She and Mrs. Hudson talked about Ohio, and the rest of us listened as General Custer told us stories of Cold Harbor and Five Forks. Then Thomas raised the question.

"General," he said, "do you suppose we might be able

to ride along with the detachment of soldiers you're sending to Ft. Laramie?"

"Who told you I was sending men to Ft. Laramie?" he
asked in turn.

"Just rumors. Bear Claw Sullivan told us we could
probably catch a train at Laramie, though," Thomas went
on to say.

"Well, it might be arranged," Custer said. "You'd have
to move fast."

"Faster than with Bear Claw?" I asked.

"Probably not," Custer laughed.

So it was settled. After attending a chapel service at the
fort, we set out behind a column of cavalry recruits for
Ft. Laramie. I learned from the men that they were to replace about thirty men who were leaving the army soon.
Jerome and I were not very impressed by them. I didn't
think the Indians would have any trouble slaughtering
the whole mess of us. Six of the soldiers couldn't even
speak English.

Nevertheless, there was a feeling of security in num-
bers. I slept better at night as we headed northwest.

III

It took us more than a week to reach the Platte River. The cavalrymen rode in a column up front, followed by their three supply wagons. We followed them. We never saw a sign of Indians, although Lieutenant Carpenter, who was in charge, told us we were watched by some Kiowas.

The Kiowas must have thought we were merely a military expedition, I thought to myself. I was not interested in changing their minds, and neither were the soldiers. Only one of the men had ever been in a battle, and that had been in Germany. Lieutenant Carpenter had been at Petersburg and the final campaign which led to Appomattox.

I spent most of my time walking along with Jerome. Thomas and Isaac were too caught up in their plans for striking it rich in California to find time for me. Each evening, Jerome and I would check our progress on a map which Lieutenant Carpenter had given me.

The days were unbelievably hot, and I was glad when we finally reached the Platte. After we forded, Jerome led Mrs. Hudson behind a clump of trees, and we stripped off our clothes and dove in the water.

If the Kiowas were still watching us, they probably thought we were all crazy. The soldiers, Mr. Hudson, Thomas and Isaac followed our lead, and soon we were all drowning ourselves in the river.

The soldiers kept to themselves, but Jerome and I jumped all over each other. He must have been a foot taller than me, but I felt fresh and alive for the first time since we had left Ft. Riley, and I was more than a match for him.

I suppose we lost half a day's traveling time that day, but even Lieutenant Carpenter agreed it was worth it. I laughed and screamed and felt young again.

After we finished our swim, we helped Mrs. Hudson wash clothes. Drying was no problem. We just hung the clothes up on ropes, and they were dried by the prairie heat.

Jerome and I saw by the map that we were to follow the Platte all the way to Ft. Laramie. We were delighted to think of an afternoon swim every day.

That night we were serenaded by one of the soldiers. He spoke only a little English, but he sang a beautiful song in German about his sweetheart. It was called "Louisa," and it told all about a lovely girl from Schleswig-Holstein.

Mrs. Hudson took him a big piece of apple pie when he finished singing. She really liked that song, and after that night, he sang it every evening for her.

As the days passed, it stayed light longer and longer. Most of the evenings we gathered around the wagon together. Mrs. Hudson took out her worn family Bible and read appropriate passages. Her father had been a minister, and she seemed to know the whole book by heart.

After she finished, I opened my box and took out one of Mother's books. They were exciting stories about great adventures and famous battles. There were some American books about George Washington, Benjamin Franklin, and people like that. My favorite was a book about knights of the round table. I would read it and then tell Jerome about it.

"I can just see some guy all duded up in armor out here," Jerome said one day. "He'd fry."

I had to agree with him, so I put the book aside and got one out about the Iroquois Indians. After a few days of that book, Jerome and I took turns terrorizing his mother with fake Indian raids.

This was finally put to a stop by Lieutenant Carpenter, who threatened to turn the rear part of us red for good. I noticed the soldiers were now detailing regular scouts, and they were posting guards at night. Lieutenant Carpenter seemed worried. I remembered what Colonel Custer had said about the Sioux and Cheyenne.

The cavalry rode in regular lines now, despite some grumbling by the men. Jerome and I still had our afternoon swim, but the soldiers took turns. Mrs. Hudson was growing very anxious, but she tried not to let it show. Only Thomas and Isaac seemed not to worry.

"Do you think the Sioux will attack?" I asked Lieutenant Carpenter one night.

"Not now," he answered. "They're north of here. I'm more worried about Cheyenne. They believe this area was promised to them as hunting grounds. They don't like whites here."

"Why do we come then?" I asked him.

"We got orders," answered Lieutenant Carpenter. "I

guess it's our way to come. The Indians will accept it for
so long. Then they'll fight. We'll win, and they'll have to
go somewhere else."

"What happens when there isn't any other place for
them to go?" I asked.

"I guess they'll either fight or go to a reservation."

"I think I'd fight," I told him.

"I guess I would, too. Their problem is that they believe our politicians. Those men from Washington come
out here and make promises. Then twenty years later they
want to make another deal."

I shook my head. I'd always thought Indians were a
bunch of naked animals. They howled and shot arrows at
you. Now I wasn't so sure. Bear Claw thought the Indians
were good. I knew what he said was usually true.

I found Thomas under a rare tree, stretched out ready
to go to sleep.

"Thomas," I asked him, "are Indians good or bad?"

He motioned me over, and I sat down on his blanket.

"Timothy," he said, "I've never seen a boy so small
with so many questions. They're bad if they shoot at us. If
they're peaceful, then they're just fine."

"Lieutenant Carpenter says it's the fault of our politicians," I told him. "I think I'd fight if a bunch of strangers
tried to take my lands."

"They don't own these lands," Thomas told me. "They
don't do anything with them. They just hunt on them. If
they really wanted the land, they'd plant on it and build
cities. They just run around naked and kill each other.
I've heard that before we came the Indians were always
at war with each other. Now they mostly fight us."

He took my hand and pulled me to him. Then he tick-
led me so that I squealed and squirmed.

"You're growing up," he told me. "We don't get to California soon, you'll be beating Isaac and me out of our
gold mine."

I knew he was just kidding, but I smiled at him. It had
been a long time since my brother had made me feel I
belonged to him.

I asked Mrs. Hudson about the Indians next. She told
me the Bible told me to love my neighbors, but she said it
also warned about heathens. Mr. Hudson made it simpler.

"They'll kill you," he said. "All you need to know about
Indians is that they'll kill you if you don't be careful."

After that, I forgot all about it. We were getting closer
to Ft. Laramie, and I decided to dream about the Rocky
Mountains.

We finally reached the forks of the Platte. The wide
rolling river suddenly turned into a muddy, wallowing
creek. We took the north fork, and although we had
plenty of water, the days we could swim were fewer and
fewer.

Almost a third of the cavalrymen stood guard every
night now. Thomas, Isaac and Mr. Hudson took turns,
too. I got some bullets for my Colt from a corporal, but
Isaac made me promise to keep them in my pocket unless
we were attacked.

We got closer and closer to Ft. Laramie. As the foot-
hills of the Rockies fell into view, we spotted our first Indians. Mrs. Hudson gasped and screamed. Jerome and I
jumped in the back of the wagon, and I loaded my gun.

There were only about a dozen of them, and I should
have known they weren't attacking. They were nearly

naked, wearing only some cloth around their waists. Some of them had feathers in their hair, and one or two of them wore necklaces of bear claws around their necks.

They met with Lieutenant Carpenter, who yelled to us not to worry. They were Crow from the fort. They wanted some trade goods, so we swapped some blankets for some fancy beadwork. One of the younger ones came over and looked with wide eyes at my Colt.

I noticed he had only three fingers on his left hand, and I asked Lieutenant Carpenter about it.

"The Crows believe they must cut off a joint from a finger to mourn a dead relative. The Crows are our allies, so they have powerful enemies. The Sioux, Cheyenne and Blackfoot are all after them. They used to hold the entire Bighorn Valley and most of central Wyoming. Now they're forced up into northern Montana for the most part."

"How come these Indians are here, then?" I asked.

"They scout for the army. They hate the Sioux, and they love to lead our soldiers against them."

"I thought all Indians were the same," I said.

"No," said the Lieutenant. "They're like different nations. The Crow and the Blackfeet have been at war since the beginning of time. One side is always raiding the other."

I didn't understand, but the Crows seemed friendly. They were all fascinated by my long blond hair. They ran their fingers through it and made a big fuss over it. When they left, I went over to Mrs. Hudson.

"Ma'am," I said, "do you suppose you could give me a haircut? Indians take scalps, and those Crows were kind of interested in my hair."

"Why sure, honey," she laughed.

Lieutenant Carpenter told me later that Crows won't attack a white man unless they have smallpox in their lodges, but I figured it didn't hurt to be sure.

The day before we were due to arrive in Ft. Laramie, Lieutenant Carpenter gave us some bad news.

"My scouts tell me the last wagon train West left yesterday. They couldn't wait for you, as they were behind already. I'd suggest you really make tracks once you get to the fort. They won't be going too fast the first few days because they don't like to get strung out in Indian territory."

We took the news soberly. I talked Jerome into a last swim in the muddy North Platte. As we splashed in the cool water, I talked to him.

"You think we can catch the wagon train, Jerome?"

"We'd better," he said. "If we don't, we'll be all alone. I think we might catch an arrow or two that way."

"I wonder what the Indians do to kids when they attack."

"You're young enough that they might try to raise you themselves. I've heard of that. Me, I'm too old. I'd be a man if I was an injun."

"You?" I asked, laughing.

"Sure," he said. "Pa says he'll have to get me a razor when we get to Oregon."

"You gonna shave your legs?" I asked.

"I got whiskers," he said, insulted. "Three or four at least."

"I heard Indians do terrible things to you," I said, changing the subject.

"They kill you," Jerome said. "Can't be much more terrible than that."

"They strip you and tie you in the sun. I heard a guy in Cairo say that. They cut the meat off you and eat it. I heard that, too. And they do all that while you're still alive."

"That's a bunch of bull," Jerome said. "They don't do things like that."

"I don't know about that. I saw one of those Crows with a scalp on his spear."

"They scalp you after you're dead," said Jerome.

"You sure?"

"Sure," said Jerome, splashing me hard.

We laughed our way into the night until Mr. Hudson told us to get out of the water and get some sleep.

When we rode into Ft. Laramie the next day, I was surprised again. Ft. Laramie was little more than a trading post. There were Indian tepees outside. Soldiers walked their posts all along the outside walls. I could tell they were nervous.

Inside, one of the Crows came over to me and felt my hair. He moved his hand over my head and grunted something in Crow talk. Lieutenant Carpenter told me the man was upset that I'd cut my hair. He said the Crows believed that blond hair was good luck. It had to do with the sun. I was sorry I'd cut it. I felt we might need some good luck.

Jerome and I reverted to our riverboat habits. We got into anything and everything on the post. The blacksmith nearly got us with a molten horseshoe, and the cook powdered us with flour. The worst happened in the stable. We were bothering a couple of guards, and one of them picked up Jerome under one arm, me under the other, and dumped us in a horse stall. The horse was gone, but we knew he'd been there. It took an hour of bathing in the river to get rid of the smell.

That night Isaac and Thomas drew me aside.

"Can't Jerome come with us?" I asked.

"No, Timothy," Thomas told me. "This is family business."

He hadn't used that phrase in a long time, and I knew it was serious.

"Timothy, we've been talking with a lot of these soldiers," Thomas told me. "They say there's a big gold strike in Colorado. Isaac and I talked it over, and we've decided to go south with them."

"But you promised to take me to Oregon first," I complained.

"We know, Timothy," Isaac said, "and if you hold us to our promise, we'll go on. But these soldiers are going now, and we're not even sure we can catch the wagon train. If we don't, we'll spend a whole year here at Ft. Laramie."

"Look, Timothy," Thomas said, "we talked to the Hudsons. They want you to go West with them. They can do as much for you as we can. You know us, we're wayfarers. We wouldn't have stayed in Oregon. I know you've been left alone too often in your young life, but the Hudsons will be like a second family to you. If you want to come south with us, though, we'll take you."

I looked with my hurt eyes at them. I hadn't spent much time with them since Ft. Riley, and they probably figured I didn't need them anymore. Something inside me needed them very much, though.

"Don't leave me all alone," I cried out, grabbing them both.

"It's okay, Timothy," Thomas said, stroking my head.

"Sure, Timothy," Isaac said. "We won't leave you."

The three of us just sat silently for a while. I was crying like a little kid, and Thomas and Isaac weren't much better. At last, I wiped away my tears and stood up.

"I'd just get in the way in a gold mine," I said. "I told Martha I'd come to Oregon. I guess I'd better go."

"Then it's settled," replied Isaac. "We'll tell the soldiers we're going to get our little brother to Oregon."

"No, it's okay," I said. "I'll go with the Hudsons. I know you've been looking out for me long enough. But you'd better get awful rich."

They both smiled at me. I don't think I got any sleep that night, staying up talking to them. It seemed strange that I should discover how much I really loved those two brothers of mine just when they were about to leave. It reminded me that I hadn't written to Helen and Joseph or Matthew and Robert since we'd left St. Louis. I got my letter written and gave it to Lieutenant Carpenter. He told me it would get out by the first messenger.

At the crack of dawn, I waved good-bye to Thomas and Isaac. I loaded up my box of possessions and stowed it in the Hudsons' wagon. Marching beside Jerome, we left Ft. Laramie headed West.

IV

We drove the wagon hard across the prairie. Mr. and Mrs. Hudson took turns driving the weary oxen while Jerome and I walked alongside. I missed Isaac and Thomas, but as we rolled along, the mountains to the west and south lit a fire inside me.

The first two days out of Ft. Laramie, our greatest danger was a rattlesnake that nearly got me. I managed to avoid it just in time. After that, I kept my Colt loaded. When Mr. Hudson found out I'd loaded the gun, though, he took the bullets away.

"Timothy, my boy," he said to me, "you and that gun are a lot more dangerous to us than any old rattler."

The third day everything changed. We were hoping to catch sight of the wagon train by then. We caught sight of something else instead, Indians.

I never figured we'd get more than a couple of days away from Ft. Laramie before running across some Indians. But I figured we'd meet the other wagons before that. On the other hand, we weren't sure we were following the trail correctly. Anyway, the Indians were there, watching from the top of a low ridge to the south. And we were all alone.

I didn't know tribes of Indians. I thought for a minute they might be Crow. I guess I hoped more than thought, though. Mr. Hudson got his rifle from the wagon and loaded it. He handed a second one to Jerome.

"Can I have my bullets?" I asked him.

"You ever fire that cannon, Timothy?" he asked me.

"No," I answered.

"Then let's wait awhile."

The Indians were dressed in deerskin leggings and brilliant feather headdresses. On their chests were some sort of bone and bead mats. Their faces wore frowns. Worse, those same faces were painted in bright reds and yellows.

I'd heard soldiers talking about painted faces. That meant the Indians intended war.

One of the Indians, I suppose it was their chief, rode his big white pony right out in front of us and raised his lance into the air. He screamed horribly.

Mrs. Hudson yelled for us to get in the wagon, and we ran. I grabbed the side of the moving wagon and pulled myself aboard. Jerome jumped on the front, and Mr. Hudson climbed up beside him.

I looked behind me and shuddered. The whole ridge was filled with Indians. There was not a sound among them, but they slowly began forming a distant circle around us. Mr. Hudson grabbed the reins and whipped the oxen. The poor beasts were not built for speed, though, and they plowed ahead.

I thought I'd been scared before, but now I knew I just thought it was fear. I couldn't seem to catch my breath. My feet shook, and I couldn't keep still. I was freezing with cold, even though it was nearly noon in the middle of the summer.

My hands fumbled their way into my pockets. I could feel the locket with my mother's picture, but the bullets for my gun were missing. I remembered Mr. Hudson had them. Shuddering, I dropped my gun, and it tumbled out of the wagon to the ground below.

Then the Indians charged. Their cries were horrible, and I tried to make my way around the outside of the wagon and get inside. Tears of horror rolled down my cheeks as I dodged a spear poked at me by a warrior. I heard a terrible scream from the front of the wagon. Then there was a terrific bang, and the wagon broke loose from the oxen.

For a moment, the wagon rolled on along on its own. I heard Mrs. Hudson shout to jump clear. Then I saw the wagon turn. I tried to jump, but my fingers refused to loosen their grip on the wagon.

There was a bang as the wagon slammed into a gully, and the wheels broke off. I felt myself tumble to the ground and stared in horror as the wagon bore down on top of me. My legs burned with pain as the wagon slid over them.

My bare back was torn by the rocky soil, and I could only manage to move sideways. In front of me a terrible scene was taking place. Mrs. Hudson dragged herself to the front of the wagon, a spear hanging from her side.

Jerome was about twenty yards in front of me, firing away at the circling Indians. Mr. Hudson stood to my left, trying to get to his wife.

Then a big warrior rode straight for Jerome. Jerome was fourteen, but he wasn't tall for his age. He tried to deflect a war club with his rifle, but the Indian struck hard. Jerome fell, the side of his head red with blood. Mrs. Hudson screamed.

Mr. Hudson tried to make his way to Jerome, but the man was struck down in front of me by three arrows. He turned toward me, blood dribbling from his lips. Then he fell, dead.

I'd never seen anyone die before, much less anyone I cared about. My eyes clouded with tears, but it didn't keep me from seeing the rest.

Jerome wasn't dead. He struggled to get to his feet, but he failed. Mrs. Hudson saw me and limped toward me. I suppose she wanted to free me, but I don't really know what good it would have done. I was terrified and unarmed. Still, I suppose it was all she could think of to do.

A young brave rode by and swung his war club at her. He missed and howled in fury. Halting his horse, he made a second run at her. This time he cracked her skull, and she rolled down the hill toward her husband.

I screamed in fury, struggling to free myself. I swallowed my tears and fought to strike back. I was firmly pinned under the wagon, though, and my efforts were fruitless.

The Indians dismounted before us now. Two of them, an old warrior and the young brave, walked over to Mr. and Mrs. Hudson. Their backs were to me, so I couldn't see what they were doing. In the back of my mind, I supposed they were scalping their victims. I hoped that was all. At any rate, their pain was over. I knew mine was just beginning.

They still ignored me, though. I thought to myself that they knew where I was. I wasn't going away. Then I saw a young man eye me. Waving his knife at me, he went instead to Jerome.

I was hoping that my friend had died by now. I didn't want him to see what they were doing to his parents. That wasn't his problem now. They pulled him to his feet right in front of me.

The left side of his face was no longer a face. It was covered with blood, and the eye was closed. There was no longer an ear there at all. Then they stripped off his clothes. Laughing, the young brave kicked him back to the ground.

Jerome was too weak to fight back.

"Why don't you kill him and get it over!" I shouted to the Indians. "He never did anything to hurt you. All he wanted was to get to Oregon."

The Indians around Jerome laughed at me. They screamed their own words back at me. Then they started on Jerome. The young Indian took a knife and cut across Jerome's chest.

"God," I said to myself, "they're going to cut off his meat and eat him. Just like the boy in Cairo told me."

That wasn't it at all. Another Indian came over and made another cut. This one started at the neck and went all the way down his body.

Jerome screamed in pain. I screamed in terror. I found myself feeling every cut they made in him.

A third Indian came over and continued the mutilation. I never knew a man could be cut so many places. They took turns cutting his body every direction possible. None of the cuts were deep enough to kill him, though, and his screams ran through the length of my body. In the back of my mind, I thought over and over the same thing. I was next.

They started on his hands next. It looked like they were cutting off his fingers. Jerome's screams grew weaker and weaker. In the end, they were little more than moans. Finally, the Indians stood up around Jerome and yelled. They raised their hands high and screamed. Then one of them took his scalp. I realized that my friend was dead. It hit me with a dull feeling in my stomach. I suddenly broke out in tears.

The next thing I knew, the wagon was being lifted from my legs. I'd already seen what they did with captives, so I squirmed from under the wagon. My legs still hurt, though, and I couldn't run far.

A big warrior leaped in front of me and waved his lance in my face. I put my head down and butted him right in the stomach. He grunted and fell backward. I grabbed his lance.

"Now come and get me!" I screamed to them, holding the big lance with both hands.

They laughed at me, but kept their distance. One charged in close, and I swung the lance at him. Another came from the other side, and I was knocked to the ground. Two of them pulled me to my feet and began tearing my clothes off.

I'd already had a demonstration of what would follow, and I started crying. I stumbled naked to the ground and looked up at them.

"Please," I sobbed. "Please don't," I cried out.

The only thing I could think of was that I was going to die out here in the middle of nowhere. I wouldn't even be nine years old. No one would even know I was dead. No one would even bury me. After the Indians were through with their sport, I'd make a good meal for a coyote or a wolf. Maybe the birds would even get some of me.

One thought suddenly made me laugh. I'd cut my hair. They wouldn't get much of that.

When I laughed, the Indians suddenly stared at me.

"That's right," I yelled at them, "you won't get much hair from me! I got it all cut off."

A tall man in a huge war bonnet then came over to me. He looked at my eyes, then grabbed me by the hair.

"Not much there." I laughed again at him. "You won't have much of a scalp for your belt."

Then I saw that the Indian next to him held in his hand the scalp of Jerome. I was suddenly flooded with memories of the riverboat, swimming in the Platte, being pitched in the horse stall. Tears rolled down my cheeks, and I struck out at the man.

"I'll kill you," I shouted, pounding my small fists in his chest. "I'll kill you."

The big man grabbed my arm and slung me over his shoulder. I screamed and pounded him. He took me to a horse and slung me over the back of it like a sack of flour. Then he yelled for the others to mount their horses and follow him.

I didn't know what they were going to do with me, but I figured that if they wanted to torture me like Jerome, they could have done it there. I looked behind me at my friend lying naked and mutilated in the summer heat. I could already see buzzards circling overhead. I didn't know what lay ahead for me, but I knew all my happiness was behind me.

V

I don't know how many miles we rode before we got to the camp of the Indians. I was frightened, and I fainted several times along the way. When we arrived, the Indians hooted and hollered at the tops of their lungs. They held their three scalps high in the air, the blood hardly dry.

The chief took me off the horse and threw me to the ground. I rolled hard against an old woman who gave me a hard kick in my side. I gasped and stared at her in pain. But that was only the beginning. I was soon left to the children, who had their own ideas about the treatment of captives.

Two boys younger than me, nearly naked, grabbed my hair and pulled me toward a group of tepees. All along the way, young boys and girls kicked me without mercy. In my nakedness, I felt ashamed and vulnerable. I tried to fight back, but they danced out of range, only to return from the other side to kick me again.

Finally, I had all I could take. Screaming loudly, I lashed out with all the fury I could muster at the two boys who were pulling my hair. I pulled myself free and then struck out at one of them.

I landed a solid blow on his face that left my right hand bleeding and sore. The boy fell away, and I turned to the rest of them.

"Ahhhhh," I screamed, knocking a small boy to the ground. "Now we'll see who can hit," I yelled to them. "I'll kill you all."

Then I felt a heavy hand on the back of my head. For a moment, things blurred. Then I fell into darkness.

I awoke to find myself inside a tepee, still naked, with a ringing sound in my ears. There was a young woman next to me who was washing my face. She smiled at me, and I tried to smile back.

"Who are you?" I asked her. "Do you speak English?"

"White man call me Dancing Dove," she said in broken phrases. "Learn speak white tongue from man with cross."

"A missionary?" I asked her.

Her eyes gave me a blank response.

"Where am I?" I asked next.

"Haha," she laughed. "Lodges of mighty Cheyenne braves. I take care you," she said, waving her hand from herself to me.

"What will they do to me?" I asked.

She smiled in a way that sent a shiver down my back. I could see she knew, but that she wouldn't tell me.

The woman ran her hands through my hair, smiling. There was a strange tenderness to her touch, and I didn't pull away. I knew too much of Cheyenne cruelty to want to fight Cheyenne kindness.

We were interrupted by the entry of a tall, broad-shouldered man clad in deerskin leggings and a fierce war bonnet. Dancing Dove moved away from me, her eyes full of terror. The big man slapped her hard, motioning with his hand for her to leave. Then his cruel eyes turned to me.

He didn't speak at all. He stood me up and looked me over. He felt the meat on my shoulders first. Then he flexed my arms and examined the muscles. He frowned. Shaking his head, he grabbed my jaw in his vicelike hands and forced my mouth open. With his other hand, he felt my teeth.

I tried with all my might to bite down on his hand, but his grip held me firmly. Then he released my jaw and turned to my legs. He spread my legs apart and felt the muscles of my thighs. Then he felt my calves. He was dissatisfied, I could tell.

Finally, he pinched my stomach. He grunted, spitting on my feet. Then he slapped my chest, sending me reeling to the ground.

"Ahhhhh," I screamed, hurling myself against him, hitting with my hands and kicking with my feet.

He just pushed me away. Then he laughed out loud, mumbling something in Cheyenne talk. Then he walked out of the tepee.

The second he left, I made a dash for it. My feet flew out of the tepee, but an old woman cornered me a few feet away.

"Ahhhhh," I screamed at her, hoping to frighten her away.

Instead, she reached out and threw me to the ground. I was quickly surrounded by children, all of them pointing at me and laughing. They took turns beating me with sticks, lashing my back and shoulders until I thought I would die. I tried to fight back, but they were too quick for me. I felt the pain bite deeper and deeper into my back. I could feel blood dribbling down my thighs.

"Ahhhhh," I screamed, jumping at the tallest of them.

He moved back three steps and then struck me in the stomach with his stick. I doubled over in pain, rolling to the ground. The children hooted and cheered, kicking dirt into my eyes.

Then there was a shout from the campfire behind me, and the children scrambled away. Looking around, I saw there were many men gathered there, dressed in great war bonnets of eagle feathers. They had their spears next to them, and I figured they were planning to attack Ft. Laramie or something. Maybe they were after the wagon train we had headed for. I didn't know and I didn't care.

I shook off the pain and sat up. I was covered with red soil, and my knees were bleeding from the hard sandstone rocks. There was blood in my scalp, and my back and shoulders were battered. My hand was swollen, and my right thigh had a three-inch gash in it.

I sat there in my nakedness and wondered what they would do next. I thought of slipping away in the darkness, but I saw that the old woman was just a few feet away, armed with a big war club. There was cruelty in her eyes, and I knew she was just waiting for a chance to strike me down.

As I began to catch my breath, I felt a rock strike my head. Then another hit my shoulder. I turned around to see the Cheyenne children. They grinned their hideous wild smiles and threw again.

"Ahhhhh," I screamed again, charging them.

I leaped at the first one I saw, grabbing his ear and

pulling him to the ground. He kicked me hard in the stomach, and I released his ear.

I struck out with all my might, landing a couple of blows to the head of one of them. They may have hit me a hundred times, but it didn't matter anymore. I was numb.

Then there was a shout like I'd never heard before. It came from the campfire, and the Cheyenne children vanished. In terror, I saw the tall warrior, covered with eagle feathers, standing tall against the pale summer sky. He was like stone, totally without movement. His left hand moved slightly, and a young Cheyenne ran quickly to me, grabbed my arm, and pulled me to them.

The big Indian reached over and lifted me by my hair off the ground. I thought my scalp would come off, and I screamed with all my might. I kicked at him. Then I tried to bite his hand. There was a circle of laughter around us as the rest of the Cheyenne enjoyed my performance. Then the man dropped me, and I rolled into a pile on the ground.

I grabbed my aching head, tears rolling from my eyes. I turned to stare with hatred at the chief. There was silence around the campfire.

Then a huge mountain of a man, clothed in bear skins, stood up. The ground trembled beneath him, and the fierce Cheyenne stood still, their eyes fixed on the man.

He walked away and returned with an arm filled with buffalo hides. A slow, rolling laughter coming from his mouth, he spoke to the chief in the language of the Cheyenne.

The chief turned to me, kicking me hard in the ribs. He told the big man something.

The man laughed and pointed to me. He laughed again.

The chief grew angry. He pointed to me and threw something on the ground.

The man just turned away, shaking his head. But the chief reached out and caught his arm. Then they smiled, and there was a loud whooping and hollering from all the Indians.

The chief walked back to me and picked me up in his huge hands. He then threw me over the fire to the huge man. I was so close to the fire that I felt the heat on my hips. The man caught me and set me down beside him. Then he motioned for me to follow.

I had no idea what was happening. The huge man was stone-faced, and I could catch no word from him. I didn't know whether I was being sacrificed, tortured or sold. The last seemed most likely since the man no longer carried the hides.

I followed him to a great brown horse. He threw a blanket to me. With his hands, he indicated I was to cover myself with it. Then he brought out another horse— a mule, really—and pointed for me to get on it.

We rode out of the Cheyenne camp, pulling three other mules along. They were filled with pelts and hides, and I was confused. As we passed out of sight of the Cheyenne fires, he turned his great bearded face toward me.

"You cook?" he asked me.

I was surprised to hear him speak English. I could see his skin was white, but he wasn't like me.

"You speak English," I said, my whole self relaxing.

"For you," he said with a twisted smile. "You cook?" he asked again.

"Some," I answered. "I have."

"You worth twenty dollars gold?" he asked.

"What?" I asked, confused.

"Just paid 'nough hides for twenty dollars gold at the fort. You better'd be worth it."

I was frightened all over again. I couldn't help but start to cry.

"Tears for squaws," he mumbled, riding away from me. "No place for tears here."

I swallowed hard and caught up with him.

"We camp tonight nearby," he told me. "You be better when morning comes."

"I'll try to be worth your money," I said, managing half a smile. "I'll try."

"You'd be a fool not to," he snarled. "Don't ride with no fools myself."

We rode on for nearly a mile. There was a stream cutting through a stand of pine there, and the man pointed to a small shelter. We removed the saddles from his horse and my mule. Then we stored the hides and furs in the shelter. At last I walked toward the shelter, ready to collapse.

"Out here," he said. "It's cooler."

I looked around me at the wilderness. I could sense the animals all around us. There was a strange sense of danger there. I thought I could still hear the bloodthirsty cries of the Cheyenne.

"Is it safe?" I asked.

"What?" he thundered.

"Is it safe to sleep out here?"

"Ha," he laughed. "Do you think any animal in his right mind would come at me? Why I'm taller than a pine tree, meaner than a bear. I've broken cougars in my bare hands, and I've touched the sky. There's not a side of this earth I've not put my feet on, and there's not a man living who's seen the better of me."

"You're a mountain man," I said.

"Every bit of one," he snarled.

I folded my blanket out and rolled up in it. I was battered and bruised from head to toe, but I'd never dreamed I'd be alive when nightfall came. There was suddenly something wonderful about just being alive. And somehow I knew tomorrow would take care of itself.

VI

It was not a peaceful night. The rest which should have come to my weary bones was lost in the midst of a hundred terrible memories my mind could not escape.

The ghosts of Jerome and his parents flooded into my dreams, reminding me first of the gentle peaceful times on the Mississippi and the adventurous trip to Ft. Laramie. But it wasn't long before I once again saw the Cheyenne.

I howled out in the night as they struck down my friend. I screamed in terror when they started after him with their knives. I shook myself awake as they held his scalp in front of my eyes.

"Boy!" I heard a rough voice shout. "Wake up, boy," I heard it say.

"Ahhhhh," I screamed, pulling away from the huge, bare-shouldered man. "Stay away from me," I told him, drawing the blanket up against me.

"It's all right," the voice protested. "No one's goin' to hurt you."

"I'll kill you," I shouted. "I'll kill you, all of you."

"Calm down," he ordered. "You ain't talkin' to no Cheyennes now."

I shook the tears out of my eyes and looked hard through the dim dawn haze.

"Who are you?" I demanded. "Where's Jerome?"

Before he could answer, I remembered Jerome's hideous, mutilated body. All I could do was collapse in tears.

"Get ahold o' yerself, boy," the man told me.

"I'm sorry," I sobbed. "I didn't mean to be so . . . so . . . unmanly."

"Nothin' o' the kind," he growled. "You was jest bein' a boy. Cain't be nothin' else in the world, 'cause that's what you is. You see them Cheyennes doin' their knifework?"

"They made me watch," I said, shaking.

"Yer jest a bit of a boy. That Cheyenne chief talks 'bout you bein' a Screamin' Lizard. Laughs about it. Ain't to be. It's jest the spirits o' yer ma an' pa an' brother bearin' on yer mind."

"They weren't my mother and father," I said.

"Weren't?" he asked.

"My father died at Shiloh."

"Where?"

"In the war."

"What war?"

"The war between the states. Mr. Lincoln's war."

"Who?"

His eyes were blank. He didn't know of these things.

"We had a war back East," I explained.

"That's another world," he told me. "That's th'other side o' the Cheyennes."

"I know," I said, wiping away a tear.

"Yer pa was killed in a war. Yer ma?"

"She died one winter. She prayed that God would take her and spare me. I guess He took her up on it."

"Must have been a brave woman."

"Yes," I said, crying again. "I miss her."

"Natural. Good to miss her."

"I'm all alone now. My brothers are in Denver. Two of them, anyway. My sister's in Oregon. The rest of my family's still in Ohio."

"Saw Ohio once," he said. "Fair farmin' land. I's from Indiana myself. Once. Now I'm a man o' the mountains. Indians call me Bear 'cause I killed one when I was first here. Only name I know anymore."

"You shot a bear?" I asked.

"Nope. Killed him. Wrestled him and broke his neck. Now they call me Bear."

"What's your real name?" I asked.

"Don't matter. Bear's only name I got anymore. You jest call me Bear. It suits me."

"I'm Timothy. I was named after my father."

"Men out here ain't named after other men. They's named fer what they is."

"I don't want to be called Screaming Lizard," I said, tears coming back to my eyes. "I'll get over the nightmares."

"Yup," he said. "A real name'll come to you, jest like mine came to me. No hurry."

"You think so?" I asked.

"Sure," he said. "Now tell me 'bout these people the Cheyennes got. Who were they to you?"

"Mr. and Mrs. Hudson from Cincinnati. Their son, Jerome," I said, coughing, "was my friend. We rode the riverboat to St. Louis together. We swam in the Platte together. We were friends."

"They walk heavy on yer soul. Indians say when a man

dies, his spirit speaks to his friends. What's the spirit askin' fer?"

"I don't know," I said. "I couldn't do anything. They had to know that. I was trapped by the wagon. Maybe they're mad because I lived, and they died."

"Spirits don't work that way," he said. "They want you to do somethin'."

"Avenge them?" I asked.

"Maybe a ma or a pa might ask that, but not jest friends."

"I don't know."

"Were they Christian folks?" he asked, making the sign of the cross.

"Yes," I said, remembering Mrs. Hudson's Bible.

"They's wantin' to be buried Christian style. You know where they lie?"

"I think so," I said. "But I don't want to go back. It'd be terrible to see them all cut up."

"Spirits won't rest till it's done. Has to be."

"Okay," I said, trembling at the thought of going back.

"Now there's th'other thing," he said.

"What other thing?" I asked.

"The cleanin' thing," he said nervously.

"What?" I asked.

"Cleanin' you up. I ain't too sure 'bout this. It's work fer a woman, and we got none. You got to be cleaned, an' I's all there is to do it."

"I can clean myself," I said, pulling away from him.

"Got to scrub the sores an' cuts," he explained. "Got to be done by someone else. It's gonna hurt powerful, an' you ain't gonna want it to happen."

"If it doesn't?"

"You'll be takin' with the ills. You get a big fire in yer head, and you'll be restin' yer bones on the mountain."

"I'll die?"

"Seen it before. Always the same."

"Okay," I said.

It was really funny. I wasn't eager to be scrubbed, but Bear was a lot less eager to do the scrubbing. We walked down to the stream side by side, naked as the day we were born. I never saw a man like him. He was six and a half feet tall, and as big around as a wagon wheel. His beard covered all of his face except for his eyes, and the rest of him was covered with long, curly black hair.

He looked to me from the front more like a bear than a man. Only the lower part of his back wasn't covered with hair. He was a mountain of a man, but when we got to the river, he was as scared as I was.

"What do I do?" I asked.

"Git in the river," he told me.

I splashed into the cool stream slowly, feeling its freshness bring new life to me.

"What now?" I asked.

"I got to clean you," he told me, holding out a big square of lye soap to me. He jumped into the water next to me, but he just stood there, afraid to move.

"Here," I said, handing him the soap.

"Now this ain't gonna work," he told me. "I's supposed to hold onto you, but I cain't. I got no way with kids. I'm goin' to hurt you fer sure."

"You said it's gotta be done," I reminded him, staring hard into his eyes.

"Right as rain," he said, standing stiff and solemn.

With his left hand, he reached around and cradled my

neck. Then he placed the other hand under my legs and pulled me to him.

"Don't know 'bout this," he said, ready to release me.

"It's okay," I said, laughing. "Just do it and get it over. I won't scream."

He started with my feet. They were broken and bruised, and he scrubbed them mercilessly. The lye burned its way into my flesh, but I didn't stir.

His soft, thoughtful eyes kept looking over at me to make sure he wasn't hurting me, and for the first time, I recognized compassion in him. He was a rough man from a rough world, but I felt more kindness and strength in him than I'd ever felt before.

He scrubbed me with the soap from head to toe. He wrestled my body around some, but I knew he was trying to be gentle. I didn't make a sound when he tore open the gash on my thigh.

Finally, he carried me out of the water and set me down on a clean blanket.

"Sit there an' dry," he told me. "Then it's time fer the herbs."

I sat there in the sun for some time. I looked myself over and saw that I'd lost a layer of skin. I was bleeding in a hundred different places, but the only really bad place was my thigh. He came and looked me over.

"The Cheyennes weren't very pleased with me," I told Bear. "They thought I was too skinny."

"You'll grow," he told me. "Never seen nothin' like it," he said, feeling the sides of my legs. "You got the feel o' newborn rabbit, smooth as fur made fer a French lady."

"I'll toughen up," I said. "I promise."

"Yup," he said. "You will. Kinda a shame, though," he

said. "Yer like a boy I once knew back in Missouri. West toughens all the softness out."

"Who was the boy?" I asked.

"My boy. Died when I went to git some new seed. He an' my woman, both o' them. Burned down the place and headed here."

"Do you miss him?" I asked.

He turned his sad eyes to face me. I read sorrow there.

"Never took it much to mind," he said. "Boy's a boy. Sooner or later's got to be a man. Man's goin' to die. That's the way o' things."

I didn't say anything more as he rubbed his sticky herb mixture over my cuts. He wiped away the blood on my thigh and poured some liquid over it. It burned and I jumped. He stopped and looked at me.

"Did I hurt you?" he asked.

"It just stung," I told him.

"Good. It'll kill what the Crow call evil odors. Make you well."

"I met some Crows at the fort," I told him.

"Proudest people alive," he said. "Handsomest, too."

"Are you a friend of the Crows?" I asked.

"I'm brother to the Crow," he said. "I took a Crow woman a few years back. Got a young buck son by her."

"Then how can you trade with the Cheyenne?" I asked. "I thought they were enemies."

"Are," he said. "But I's strong medicine. Man kills a bear with his hands, that's strong spirit. Blackfeet leave me alone, and they're twice as bad as Cheyenne."

"Why don't you have your wife here with you?" I asked.

"She's Crow, stays with her people on the Big Horn. Cheyenne'd kill her."

"Then why do you leave her? I'd think you'd want to stay with your family."

"Ain't much use fer family here," he said. "I got no use fer her most o' the time. The boy'll learn the ways of his grandpa, who's a chief. When it's time fer him to come to me, he will."

"You don't miss them?"

"I's a mountain man. Don't need nothin'."

"Will I ever be a mountain man?" I asked him.

"Don't know," he said, finishing with his herbs. "I think maybe yer a different kind o' man."

We stayed at the camp for two days. Each night the dreams came to me, and I screamed into the night. Each time, Bear shook me awake and told me things would be all right soon. He tried to ignore me, but he came more and more to ask about me. He repeated the cleaning process each day, and his touch grew gentler.

There was a need within him for me, and I felt in his strong hand more of a father than I'd ever known.

The fourth day came early. The sun had scarcely burned away the haze when Bear shook me awake.

"Stand up fer me, boy," he said.

I laid aside my blanket and stood naked in front of him. It had made me feel ashamed and defenseless in front of the Cheyennes, but it didn't seem to matter with Bear. He went inside the shelter and brought forth wonder for my eyes.

First, there were two deerskin mocassins. I slipped my feet into them, and they fit. They were slightly big, but I would grow. I looked up at him with warm eyes.

"Thanks, Bear," I said. "They're wonderful."

"Hard part's next," he said.

He took out a deer hide and fit it to my hips. I expected it to be rough and hard, but it was soft, though rugged. Bear took his knife and cut it to fit. Then he shaped a vest.

"These will suit you till winter," he said. "By then, I'll know yer shape better."

He took the deerskin and sewed up the sides. Then he told me to put them on, and he disappeared into the shelter.

The clothes fit well. I marveled at the way I looked. The deerskin trousers and the mocassins were perfect. The vest shielded my back, but left my chest and arms bare for comfort.

I looked over at him, my eyes alive with happiness. I saw he held a hat in his hands.

"I found this a long time ago," he said. "It's likely to be big, but you'll grow to it. When we git to yer wagon, we'll find some o' yer own things. Then you can shed these. I remember how things were in Indiana, though, an' I wouldn't have been too comfortable wearin' a blanket."

"Thanks," I told him.

"You'll pay me back," he said, turning his back to me.

We rode out on the prairie. I told him what the mountains had looked like, and he took us straight to the spot. The wagon rested on its side. The three bodies lay where they'd fallen.

I jumped from my mule and raced to them. I took a stick and beat a bird away from Mrs. Hudson. They'd picked at the bodies. It was a horrible sight to see.

"Get some blankets," Bear yelled to me. "Don't look at 'em. The spirits won't ever go away then."

I ran to the wagon and searched for blankets. Blankets were of use to the Cheyenne, though, and there were none left. I took instead some dresses that belonged to Mrs. Hudson, and we wrapped them in these. Bear began digging, and I stripped planks from the wagon to use as crosses.

I carved their names on the crosses, getting the Christian names of Mr. and Mrs. Hudson from their family Bible. We buried all three and covered their graves with rocks. Bear explained this was to prevent wolves from digging them up. When we'd finished, I felt better.

"Is there anything here you want to take?" Bear asked me, sweat dripping from his beard.

"It would sound silly," I said.

"What is it?"

"There are some books of my mother's. I'd like to take them. And my father's gun."

"Take both," he told me. "And clothes, if you like."

I ended up taking everything of mine. Bear suggested I take some of Jerome's clothes, as I'd soon outgrow mine. But I knew the spirits would only be worse, and Bear agreed.

We rode away slowly, and I fought to control the tears I felt coming. I cried softly that night, and Bear came over.

"We'll be heading up to the Wind River soon," he said. "They call it that because the valley there whines like the wind. I hear yer sorrow, and it speaks to me the same way. I think I've found a name fer you."

"Not now," I said. "I'm crying. I'm not like this. Wait for me to kill a wolf."

"It's not yer way to seek a name. The name seeks you. Yer like the wind, blowin' in from the east. You come to me jest like the wind. You mourn fer yer life, jest like the wind. You should be called 'Wind.'"

I looked in his eyes and saw that he believed it. It was, after all, better than "Screaming Lizard" for a name. It was also better than being called "boy" for the rest of my life. I agreed to it.

VII

My new name and I followed Bear west. There were sights there which my eyes had never imagined. Mountains stretched so tall they swallowed the sun. Trees bigger around than even Bear. It was a wonderland of virgin land, just waiting for my feet to explore.

The long trek to the Wind River was not an easy one. Southern Wyoming was a flat, arid land. Between the mountains to the south and the mountains to the west was a flat prairie that was known as the Great American Desert.

Bear told me it was a foolish name for the place since the Indians hunted huge herds of buffalo there. There were abundant grass and small game. But the water was scarce, and we sometimes traveled days without seeing a living soul.

The sun beat down on us all day, and I was caked in dust. We ran low on water, and I dreamed of splashing in the cool waters of the Platte. One time Bear had to hold me back from drinking at a bad water hole. He explained there was too much salt in the water, and it would have made me very sick.

Our clothes were ill-suited to the heat. Bear wore only

his deerskin trousers, and I wore only mine, with the legs rolled above my knees.

The sun failed to mark Bear's brown leatherlike shoulders, but mine it baked red and raw. I had to sleep on my stomach because of the tenderness.

When we finally reached the river, Bear warned me never to stray far from him. The Shoshoni who lived there were ill-tempered at times, and they might kill a white boy on sight if it suited them. I had no intention of going far, though. As soon as I could get out of my clothes, I plunged into the river.

I must have stayed in the river half the day. It was wonderful to be clean again, and I thought to myself that I probably polluted the river permanently with all the dust I carried on my back. Bear rubbed his herb mixture on my shoulders that night, and they improved.

We camped on the river for three days. Bear said he wanted to give the mules a rest. I figured he probably wanted to rest me, too. I knew he wintered in the mountains, and it would be no easy journey through the Shoshoni.

When we were ready to start our journey again, I helped load the mules. When we finished, Bear came over to me and hoisted me up on my mule.

"Wind, you never been in the land of the Shoshoni," he told me.

"No," I said. "Never."

"Shoshoni don't take to havin' kids talk much. Not like the Crow. If we meet up with Shoshoni, and we're likely to, you keep yer words to yerself."

"I will," I told him.

It didn't take us long to find the Shoshoni. More truthfully, it didn't take them long to find us. We rode along the river for maybe two hours when we came across a group of them on horseback, blocking our way. A tall, solemn young man in the center rode out in front.

He screamed something at Bear, and Bear raised his right hand. Bear handed me the reins of the pack mules and rode forward. The young Shoshoni called out to Bear, and once again Bear raised his hand. Finally, the Shoshoni raised his hand also, and I sighed with relief. They spoke Shoshoni words, moving their hands back and forth, up to the sky, over the river, to me and the mules, and then back to themselves. Finally, Bear turned and rode to my side.

"Shoshoni camp's just ahead," Bear said. "We're welcome to stay with them. Just as well. Yer cookin' ain't so good as I figured it'd be."

"I've never cooked any of this stuff," I complained. "In Ohio, we had carrots and potatoes and corn. I never even saw any of this root stuff before."

"I know, Wind," he said, smiling. "But you watch them Shoshoni squaws. They can make river mud taste good."

When we arrived at the camp, I was set upon by all the women. They ran their hands through my hair, and I returned their friendly smiles. The children were as hard as the Cheyenne children, but after I hit one of them back, they left me alone.

One of the young warriors came over to me and pointed to my hair. I smiled at him and nodded my head, thinking he was complimenting me. Then he pulled out his knife, grabbed my head firmly in his strong arms, and cut off a lock of my hair.

I screamed and scrambled away. Bear ran over and got

between us. He said something to the Shoshoni, and the man stopped. Then he turned to me.

"What you tryin' to do, Wind?" Bear yelled at me. "Scream yer way to an early grave?"

"He cut off my hair," I said, pointing to the lock of blond hair the Shoshoni clutched in his hand.

Bear turned to the Shoshoni and talked to him. Then he turned back to me.

"You didn't understand the sign he made to you," Bear explained. "He wanted a lock o' yer hair fer his medicine pouch. He'll give you a gift in return."

"Well, he sure never said anything about cutting it off," I said. "You suppose all of them will be wanting some?"

"I'll tell them you will offer no more, in honor of this warrior. That may not exactly be true, but it'll keep th'others away and save this man from loss o' pride."

"Okay with me," I said. "What should I do?"

"Go over to that buck and hold your hand out in the peace sign. Then stand still. He'll give you somethin'. Now, Wind, I know yer a gentle type, but whatever the man hands you, you smile real big and take it."

"What if it's a scalp or something? What if it's bloody?"

"Take it, boy. You don't, he may hand you yer own scalp instead."

"I understand," I said, shaking slightly.

I walked over to the man and held out my hand. I stood just as still as I could, putting on my bravest look.

The man grunted at me, scowling his hardest. I wanted to turn and run, but I didn't. Instead, I grunted back at him. His eyes lit up, and he broke into a smile. Then he grabbed me in his big, strong arms and carried me off to his lodge.

I tried to squirm away from him, but the terror of my situation had paralyzed me. I found myself standing inside his lodge facing his wife. They talked for a moment. Then she took out a beautiful shirt woven from some kind of cloth. It bore a beautiful design on the front, and it was a marvel to behold.

He held it out to me, and I took it in my hand. I smiled at the woman and then at him. Then I raised my hand again in the peace sign and walked out, searching with my eyes for Bear.

The big man ran to me, picked me up, and took me to where our mules were tied.

"That's about the prettiest piece of goods I ever seen in a Shoshoni camp," he said. "It's a shirt fer a great warrior. You must've impressed that buck mighty much. It's about big enough fer you and another you now, but you'll grow."

"I know I'll grow, Bear," I said to him. "You don't have to remind me of it every day."

"Not you I's remindin'," Bear said with a smile. "It's me."

I reached over and knocked his hat right off his head.

"I'm not so little as you think," I told him.

"No?" he asked, grabbing me and slinging me over his shoulder. "You'd make about five seconds' worth o' breakfast fer a grizzly bear."

For just a moment, I thought he was really happy. Then he set me back down and turned away.

Much happened to me between the time we first camped on the Wind River and the coming of winter. As the first snows sprinkled on our shoulders, I realized I was nine years old. I was less of a boy and more of a man than I would have thought possible two months before.

The first thing Bear taught me was how to fish. There were no iron hooks like we had in Ohio. A thorn might be shaped into a hook, but Bear preferred to carve his own from pine saplings.

He showed me how to make a barb in the end of the hook to hold the fish. Then he set me to practicing. It was not enough to hook the fish, Bear taught me. It was important to pull hard so that the barb caught the fish.

"Then there's the Crow way," he told me.

He made two sharp wooden spears and led the way to the river.

"When you see a trout, wait fer him. As he comes at you, strike hard and quick like this," he shouted, plunging the spear into the river. He pulled the spear out with a trout wiggling in the middle of it.

I tried it with the spear, but I mostly managed to get an awful lot of Wind River mud in my ears. The trout were pretty safe from my spear. By the first snowfall, though, I'd caught my share.

Just as my fishing had improved, so had my cooking. I'd watched Helen cook fish at home, so I knew how to clean and fillet them. Even I thought they tasted good, and Bear nearly went wild.

"This fish is good eatin', Wind," he said. "Believe I could get fat on them fish."

"You're fat enough," I told him. "Maybe I'd better burn them tomorrow."

"You sure have picked up a smart mouth," he said. "Brings to mind them Crow kids. They's always pesterin' you an' botherin' you. Cheyenne or Shoshoni would belt 'em where they need it. Crow just smile."

My next lessons went better. I was eager to learn to trap, and I paid careful attention to the snares Bear built. He was more wary of teaching me to work with the big metal traps with their jagged teeth.

"Nothin' funny 'bout these," he scowled. "They can take a hand off you."

"They're all you can use for beaver, though. Right?" I asked him.

"Right you are," he said. "So take care, and always make sure you tell me where you place 'em."

Bear showed me how to bait the traps, too. I always figured he used some kind of food, but Bear used a liquid he called smell. It was named correctly, for it was the worst smelling stuff I'd ever come across. I couldn't imagine why an animal could be attracted by it, but it worked.

When we caught our first beaver, he showed me the gland he got the smell from. It was hard for me to watch Bear cut that animal all up, but I swallowed hard and learned how. By early winter, I was doing it myself.

The third and most important lesson for me was how to shoot. I knew there would be a time when both our lives would depend on my being able to fire a gun. But I was small, and it was difficult.

Bear had three guns. The buffalo gun and the big elk gun were forgotten. I could hardly lift them, and Bear told me the recoil would likely kill me. I settled for an army rifle. I didn't ask him where it came from. It was still shiny, so I figured he traded it off a Cheyenne. It was needless to ask where the Cheyenne got it.

I still had my pistol, of course, but I had only seven bullets for it. Besides, Bear told me, it wouldn't be much use against an animal.

We started my shooting lessons on a cool morning. We were camped away from the river, and Bear made me carry the gun myself. It was heavy, and it took all my strength. When I set it down or tried to drag it, he scolded me.

"Lift it, Wind," he hollered. "Carry it."

I did my best. When we got to a place that satisfied him, he put some pine cones on a log and returned to me. He showed me how to prime the gun, then how to load it. When he was satisfied that I wouldn't blow my head off, he told me to aim for the pine cones.

I tried to hold the long gun steady, but it nearly tipped me over. I finally got down on one knee and braced the barrel on a tree limb. I sighted the gun on the last pine cone on the right and pulled the trigger.

The explosion knocked me backward, and I rolled into a heap.

"Great shot!" Bear yelled. "Natural mountain man, this boy."

I looked up and saw that the cone on the left was blown to pieces.

"Got to tell the truth, Bear," I said. "I was aiming at the one on the right."

"Oh," he sighed. "Well, back to work."

The first day, I fired three times. After that, my shoulder was too sore to hold the gun, and we returned to camp. But after two weeks, I could carry the gun up a mountain. And if I braced the gun on something to hold it steady, I could hit pretty well what I wanted.

One night when we were sitting together around a roaring campfire, he told me about the Crow.

"This river winds around to the north, you know," he

said. "They call it the Big Horn up there, and the Crow camp in its valley. Crow's a fine people. Honest, brave, friendly."

I smiled as he went on. Then I reached my small hand over and touched him on his huge, bearskin-covered shoulder.

"What'd you do that fer?" he asked, looking at me with confused eyes.

"I don't know," I said. "I never did it before."

"Then why?" he asked.

"I don't know," I repeated. "I guess it's 'cause I like you."

"You do?" he asked.

"I do," I said. "Back home I used to touch my sister-in-law, Helen. She was soft and smooth, and it was nice to touch her."

"I ain't nice and soft, an' especially not smooth," Bear growled.

"I know," I told him. "It's kind of different with you. I never knew my father, or I guess I'd know how it's supposed to be. I guess it's pretty silly for me to do. It's a kid thing to do."

"Yer a kid," Bear said. "Kids do kid things."

"I've got to grow up fast," I said. "I'm going to be a mountain man."

"Cain't rush nature," Bear said. "Boys grow fast enough. Fast as they's intended to."

We didn't talk about it anymore, but I knew I did have to grow up fast. I had to be able to help out. I had to be able to take care of myself.

Our last camp before the mountains was beside a Shoshoni village. I was dressed in dearskin pants and shirt, and I wore a coat of fox fur. They kept me warm, and I told myself I looked less like Timothy Welles from Ohio and more like Wind.

Bear was pleased with the way I looked. I figured the Shoshoni took me to be his son, and I don't think it shamed him as it might have in the camp of the Cheyenne.

When night fell, we sat around our campfire and gazed at the stars.

"When will we go into the mountains?" I asked Bear.

"Soon. I have a cabin in the Tetons. It's solitary up there. You can look down on the rest of the world. Lots o' game there in the winter. Mostly elk. Then there's the Teton Sioux, the Gros Ventres, and the Blackfeet. They keep you company."

"I heard the Sioux and the Blackfeet are mean," I said.

"Meanest. Gros Ventre are cousins o' the Crow, but they's mean, too. They don't go up Bear's mountain, though. Feared o' spirits there."

There was a sound in the woods behind us, and we turned quickly to see what it was. Bear pulled out his knife, and I grabbed my Colt.

"Friends," a voice called out. "We come of God."

Bear put aside his knife, and I looked at him with surprise. Out of the darkness came an old man and a young woman.

"We come in peace," the man said, sitting across the fire from us. "Prudence heard voices speaking English, and we thought we might have a chance to visit with you."

"My fire's always open to any who come in peace," Bear said. "Who be you?"

"I am Reverend Hollis Ramsey from Philadelphia," the man said. "This is my daughter, Prudence. We've come

West to help the heathens learn the true light of the Lord."

"Most o' these heathens behave themselves a whole lot better than men do in Philadelphia," Bear told the man.

"I'm afraid that's true," the reverend said. "But when they learn to read and write and understand our laws, they will come to understand us. They will be civilized."

"Well, yer doin' what you think's right fer 'em. They been here thousands o' years. Don't s'pose you can ruin 'em in a few lifetimes."

"Perhaps we'd best be going," the woman said. "It appears we're not welcome."

"Not at all, ma'am," said Bear. "Just so we understands each other. I's a man o' the mountains. I know the spirit o' the clouds you call God. He knew me before I came West, and I know Him now I's here. It's enough fer me to understand."

"You call Him a spirit," said the young woman. "Don't you call Him God?"

"Don't see it hardly matters," Bear frowned. "If He's the one I know, and the one you know, then He's th'only one there is anyhow."

"How strangely logical," said the reverend. "And what of you, boy? Do you know God, or has your father brought you up worshiping totems?" the man said to me.

"Bear is not my father," I said. "But what he's taught me has always been true."

"You speak like an easterner," observed the reverend. "How long have you been out West?"

"Forever," I said.

"I bought him off the Cheyennes," Bear said. "That was in the summer. He's his own man now."

"What's your name, boy?" asked the woman.

"Wind," I said.

"Don't you remember your Christian name?" she asked. "How horrible. This boy in the hands of such a savage."

"I remember everything," I said. "It suits me," I said softly, looking at Bear, "to be called Wind."

His eyes smiled their approval, and I felt warm inside.

"We must go now. We'll be opening a school here soon. I doubt you care for the welfare of the boy, sir," snarled the minister. "But if you do, you might perhaps leave him with us. Perhaps there's a chance of saving him yet from going wild."

"I'll think on it, reverend. Surely will," said Bear.

After they left, a great silence filled the air. Bear was frozen in meditation. I was concentrating on him. Then he stirred.

"Wind, you will stay with the reverend," he said at last.

"I will not," I protested. "My place is with you."

"It ain't the way o' the mountains to take no boy through winter. I'd planned on sendin' you to some trappers in the Yellowstone Valley. They'd git you to yer sister in Oregon."

"No!" I shouted.

There was silence again for some time. Bear's eyes stood fixed on me, his lips uttering nothing. Finally, I spoke up.

"Why?" I asked.

"Little cub like you'd have a rough time here in winter."

"I haven't been worth twenty dollars gold to you yet," I said. "You'd be getting cheated."

"Close enough to twenty," he said sourly. "You been a good companion."

"Bear," I said, "I'd rather die here with you than go anywhere else. All my life I've been shuttled off to some relative. Even to mere strangers like the Hudsons. Don't you send me away, too."

"It'd be fer yer own good, boy," he said.

"You don't believe that," I said. "I belong with you. You told me my name chose me. Maybe my life chose me, too. Maybe it was meant to be for me to come to you. If I was meant to go back East, I'd never have come this far."

"There's truth there," Bear said.

"Please," I asked, tears coming to my eyes.

"Ain't much kind o' life fer a kid," he told me.

"I'll grow." I smiled. "I promise."

"Believe you will," he said, smiling.

I reached my arms around him and hugged him tightly. The way I'd wanted to hug the father I'd never known. I dried my tears and looked up at him.

"If you'd take to winter in my lodge, I'd have you, Wind," he said.

"I would," I answered.

"Won't be an easy time."

"I know," I said.

"I cain't be all you wants me to be," he said. "Cain't be no ma an' pa to you. Ain't in me."

"You've already been more pa to me than I've had before."

"Ain't in me," he repeated.

I turned from him and went to bed. I felt in my heart it was very much in him. It had to be. I needed it to be in him.

VIII

A fine carpet of snow covered the valley the day we prepared to leave the Shoshoni village. I was busy packing the mules and didn't even notice Bear's disappearance. When I strapped the last of the furs on a mule, I called to him.

"They're ready, Bear," I said. "We can leave."

I was greeted with silence, and an eerie feeling started down my spine. My fingers nervously tied the mules to a tree. Then I set out to find him.

The snow was heavy, and it wasn't difficult to see his footprints. I sighed in relief as I saw he'd walked toward the Shoshoni camp—alone. He'd return soon. There was probably some departing ceremony I didn't know about.

I found a log to sit on and traced my name in the snow. It was pleasing to see letters again. I'd almost forgotten there was such a thing as written language. Since I'd been with Bear, I'd not seen anything written down except the names in the Hudsons' Bible.

"Well, yer workin' hard I see," Bear snorted at me from behind. "I could just as well have lifted yer scalp, you crazed boy."

"You old mountain man," I said, turning to face him.

But I didn't finish. Instead, I stood up, frozen speechless by what he had brought.

"Well?" Bear asked me.

"Is he for me?" I asked, walking over and stroking my hand across the nose of the prettiest Indian pony I'd ever seen.

"You don't expect me to ride it, do you?" Bear asked, laughing.

"You probably paid more for him than you did for me," I said. "I'll make it up to you."

"Know you will," he said. "Besides, horses make good trade goods here. Horse can always be bought or sold."

"Boys can't be, huh?"

"Most won't put up with boy critters. They's too hard to tame."

I laughed at him.

"You haven't tamed me yet, huh?" I asked him.

"Ain't my way. Takes the spirit out o' animals to tame 'em."

When we set out for the mountains, I discovered there was a world of difference between riding a mule and an Indian pony.

I'd ridden a few horses before, but they'd always been worn-out nags. This horse was full of spirit, and it was all I could do to control him.

"Wouldn't be surprised to find that pony ridin' you 'fore we git to the mountains," Bear said, laughing.

"You'll see," I answered. "He's doing just fine."

"Know it," said Bear. "Was you I's worried 'bout."

The horse and I both made it to the mountains. I called him Sunrise because he always seemed to snort and storm when the sun came up. It was a peculiar thing for a horse to do, but it, endeared him to me.

I'd never seen anything like the snow in the mountains. Bear told me the Tetons were the most beautiful mountains in the world.

"There are mountains in Asia they say that block the sun," I told him.

"I've been everywhere," Bear told me. "I've seen all there is in this world. There are no grander mountains."

"How do you know?" I asked him. "They may be grander."

"Listen when I say, Wind, that there are no grander. I'd be there if they was. I've a mountain spirit, and it takes me to the grandest of all mountains."

I couldn't argue further with him. There was a sureness in his tone born of experience. Though neither of us ever did see the Asian mountains, I took his judgment to be the truth.

Bear's mountain was among the northern Tetons. There were a couple of taller ones to the south, but Bear's mountain was no less grand. It overlooked a river called the Snake. I saw how it got its name. The river wound its way through the valley like a sidewinder. There was never a section of it that was straight for very long.

There was much work to be done on the mountain before the heavy snows set in. The cabin had fallen into a poor state during Bear's absence, and that came first. Then we had to lay in a supply of firewood. The skies were torn with the sound of Bear's huge two-bladed ax ripping at the pines and spruces.

Bear chose carefully the trees he cut. He never cut two

side by side. Often he'd take a tall tree with smaller ones beside it.

"The smaller ones will grow tall now," he explained.

My part of the work was to gather kindling. He gave me a small ax and showed me how to strip the branches from the big trees. It took us nearly a week to repair the cabin and stack the firewood.

We next prepared the skin shed. Bear didn't like to keep the furs, especially the fresh ones, in the cabin with him. There was a shed out back for that purpose. It was mostly underground, and the ceiling beams had collapsed. It was hard work to brace them back into place. When we were finished, it was as cozy a place as there was.

We put the furs and the hides in there. Bear skillfully covered the entrance. Any thief would pass the place without knowing it was there.

The next task was to build an animal shed. It was to be like the fur shed, but this one had to be built from scratch. We dug snow and rocky soil for two days. Then we braced the walls with timbers. Finally, we cut the roof beams and laid them side by side. Last of all, we added a roof covering of soil and grass.

Sunrise and the mules were delighted with the shed. It was much warmer than the side of the mountain, and I knew the survival of the mules and horses was important to us. Even Bear's old horse, who was always called simply "Horse," seemed to delight in his new home.

Now that we were finally settled in, we set out the traps. Bear explained to me that we would probably go after elk in a few weeks.

"Elk's good eatin', Wind," he said. "They got good

strong coats, too. We need to git you somethin' better'n a buffalo hide or a fox fur."

The buffalo hide was warm, but it was nothing compared to the great bearskin Bear draped around him. The fox had been put away after the first heavy snow. When it got really cold, my teeth would chatter in the night. At those times, Bear would walk over and put the bearskin over me.

I knew on those nights, he suffered the cold instead of me, but I knew that the gift he made to me brought him a kind of happiness I would not deny him.

I suppose a month of winter passed without trouble. Bear would often take me to the bottom of the mountain and hide with me, watching the life in the valley below. He showed me parties of Gros Ventres and Teton Sioux. In the other direction, we once saw a party of Blackfeet.

Then one day we noticed our traps were empty more than usual. We knew they'd been triggered, but only gnarled remains of the animals were left.

"Somethin's raidin' our traps, Wind," Bear told me. "I'll stay with 'em tonight and find out."

"Me, too," I said.

"There's not enough warmth in you to take a winter's night in th'open," he told me. "'Sides, yer like as not to want to shoot at it in the dark. Might be a Sioux or a Gros Ventre. Might be a white man. Not worth killin' a man to stop him raidin' traps."

I didn't think this was true. I saw in his eye the first time we spotted the empty trap that he would kill whoever or whatever was doing this. But he was right about the cold. I stayed in the cabin.

The next morning, the riddle was solved. It was a grizzly bear.

"Got to kill it," Bear spoke. "I am brother to the bear, and I hate like fire to do it. Got to be done, though. Griz'll hunt man if he's hungry. Make a nice meal out o' you, Wind."

"He could eat all winter off of you," I laughed at him.

"Wind," he said seriously, "I want you to stay in the cabin. Griz is mean. They kill you awful easy."

"I'm going," I said.

"Cain't be," he said, taking his huge buffalo gun and closing the door. Before I could scramble through, he barred the door from the outside.

Bear was a big man, and brave as well. But I knew better than he did that if that bear got him, I wouldn't last much longer. I unlatched the window and slid out into the snow. I wriggled my way through the deep drifts, losing the army rifle in the process.

There was no longer any use in my going on. The gun wouldn't have been much good against a grizzly bear anyway, of course, but Bear would be right in getting after me for going out unarmed.

Still, something drove me to do it. I followed Bear's tracks in the snow, feeling something was about to happen. There was a fear in me, but it wasn't fear for myself. It was fear for him.

I floundered a number of times in the deep snow. The cold was all around me, but it didn't penetrate my skin. There was danger and worry in me, and no room for cold.

Suddenly I heard a great roar. Then there was a shot. Then a second roar split the air like thunder. It was a human roar, and terrible to behold.

I ran forward through the snow, my small legs fighting their way. At last I came to a clearing. There they were, the massive grizzly and Bear.

Bear had his great bulky arms around the grizzly, and the beast growled furiously. There was terrible peril for my friend.

I saw the buffalo gun lying in the snow in front of me. The powder horn and cartridge sack were there, too, so I ran to them. The grizzly was only feet away, but Bear still held his grip. There was fury in their movements, and I doubted Bear could hold on long.

I primed the piece and rammed down the ball. I'd seen Bear do it a hundred times, and I did it the same way. There was a strong branch in front of me, and I braced the huge gun on that. I took my time to aim it, knowing I'd have but one chance. The grizzly stood tall in front of me, but Bear was there, too. I feared I'd make the wrong shot. Then the beast swung a paw and caught Bear on the jaw. The man fell backward, and my blood ran cold.

"Kill him, will you, devil beast!" I screamed out. "Come here!"

The grizzly turned to face me. Bear lay motionless on the ground. I supposed the bear was ready for me. As the bear came closer, I fired the gun.

The air around me exploded. Snow and branches fell from the trees overhead. I was thrown backward by the blast I'd never considered.

The gun flew away from me, and I rolled over on my side. Blood trickled from my forehead, and a great throbbing pain filled my shoulder. Still, I managed to get to my feet and see to the grizzly.

The great animal lay quiet, its chest blown apart.

There was still a tremor of life in it, though, and I took my knife out. My right arm was of no use to me, so with my left, I cut the beast's throat. There was a stillness to the creature, and I dropped the bloody knife in the snow.

I found Bear still frozen in the snow. His face was covered with blood, and there were deep slashes on his legs.

"Are you dead, Bear?" I asked him, tears rolling down my face.

"Fool question if I ever heard one," he moaned. "You expect me to answer yes?"

I smiled and threw myself into his great arms.

"Don't ever leave me behind again," I told him. "It's better to die bravely together than live apart in loneliness."

"You surely did save the bacon." Bear smiled. "You got heart, boy."

Wiping blood away from his eyes, he gave me a smile.

"I killed a bear when I was nigh twenty, Wind," he told me. "But you killed one 'fore you was even ten."

The smile fell from his face as he looked at me closely. Washing the blood from his face with a handful of snow, he lifted me firmly onto his knee.

"You shouldn't never have tried to fire off that gun," he told me. "It's likely killed you. Why yer whole side is stove in."

"It didn't matter," I said. "I need you. I couldn't have made it through a winter alone."

"There's right in what you say," he said. "But it don't make it less of a thing."

Bear wasn't hurt so much after all. There was a deep slash across his cheek which bled for a while, but his legs were tough as rawhide. He just pounded some snow into the cuts and saw to me.

When Bear took off my shirt, I saw my shoulder and chest were bruised and bloody. One of my ribs was loose, and two others were blue and misshapen. There was a limpness filling my being, and I grew cold. My eyes became moist, and I looked up into Bear's cold, empty eyes.

"You'll bury me on the mountain, won't you?" I asked. "Put lots of rocks over my grave. You'll miss me, too, won't you?"

"Nothin' to miss," he said, the words tearing at me.

"Nothing?" I asked.

"You'll be up huntin' elk next week," he said.

I didn't believe him, nor did I think he did himself. But I was suddenly tired and cold, and I passed into a sleep I took for death.

I was quite surprised to wake the next morning. I thought I was dead, but Bear's bandaged face brought me a very mortal breakfast.

"Got some broth fer you," he told me. "You cain't eat no bear meat fer a few days, but it'll keep. Too cold up here to spoil."

"Are you all right?" I asked him.

"Just a scratch or two. Or twenty. You busted yerself up but good. Three ribs and a shoulder. Be most of a month 'fore you get around."

"It'll be all right, though?"

"Yer young. Them ribs can be sticky. But young-uns seem to mend right. Don't worry," he told me.

"Thanks, Bear," I said. "You saved my life."

"Did the same yerself, Wind. Wouldn't have been around to do it otherwise."

There was a new feeling between us after that. He never forbid me to do anything he did or go anywhere he went. Best of all, I too had a bearskin coat. We made it much larger than I was. It was big enough for Thomas or Isaac. I supposed I'd grow as tall as them, and I wanted the coat for me later as well as now.

Bear made me a present of a beaver hat. It, too, was warm, and I had a winter outfit made for a mountain man, even if I was the junior size.

I grew quite fond of bear meat. We must have eaten a month off that big grizzly. When it was gone at last, I turned to Bear.

"I guess I'll have to hunt down another bear," I said.

"Wind, bears ain't fer huntin' up here. They's mean fer one thing. Fer 'nother, Indians hold 'em sacred. We don't hunt bears less they hunt us."

I understood. So I got used to elk steaks and venison stew. It was good meat to grow on, and when my ribs healed, I was taller and stronger than ever.

IX

The winter snows piled higher and higher against the side of the cabin. We no longer journeyed to the south to hunt the elk. We had meat enough for the winter, and the horses did not find the going easy.

I spent most of my days working the pelts from our traps. Bear spent most of his time checking the traps near the river. The cold had grown worse, and the journey to the river by foot was a difficult one. Though I chose not to admit it, Bear and I both knew it was beyond me.

I had added to my outfit some new boots, my feet having outgrown the moccasins Bear had made for me. I also added a necklace of bear claws, made myself from the grizzly I'd killed. I was very proud of that necklace, and Bear used to make fun of it.

"You'd part with yer hair 'fore you'd part with that bunch o' claws," he'd say.

It was about the truth. I wore the necklace to sleep, covering myself with the great bearskin coat. It seemed that grizzly was protecting me now.

I was at work one snowy morning in front of the cabin skinning a rather scrawny squirrel Bear had brought me when I heard a stirring in the woods. I pulled out my Colt and nervously studied the underbrush.

Out of the trees rode a fierce-looking Indian clothed in a buffalo hide. Over his head he wore the skin of a wolf, and his eyes were red with fire. He raised his spear and fixed it lightly in his right arm. I shook with terror.

"Who you?" he demanded, aiming the spear at my heart.

"The man who will kill you," I told him, cocking the Colt.

"You have name?" he asked.

"They call me Wind," I said. "Remember it when you sing your death chant."

"You know much," he said. "Where Bear?"

"He's gone," I said. "You know him?"

"He is brother to Crow," the man answered.

Then with a movement as quick as lightning, he slipped over the side of his horse, pinned my coat to a tree with his spear, and held his knife against my throat.

"I ask last time," he said. "Who you?"

"Wind," I said. "Kill me if you will. I'll not tell you where Bear is."

"You know Bear?" he asked with harsh eyes.

"I am his friend," I said, shaking. "I hunt with him."

"You?" He laughed. "You would make poor sport for Crow."

"You are Crow?" I asked. "You look Blackfoot to me."

"You know nothing," he growled, twisting my hair. "Blackfoot scalp you by now. Crow brother to Bear. Marry sister."

"You could be lying," I said. "Bear told me never to trust an Indian."

"You tell where Bear," he demanded, holding the knife hard against my throat. "Or die."

"No," I mumbled, half choking from the grip he had on my throat.

Then I kicked him hard on the shin and slipped away. Picking up my Colt, I aimed it at his head and fired. The bullet shattered a tree limb beside his head, and he froze.

"Now tell me who you are," I shouted. "Maybe you'd like to die."

"What's goin' on here?" bellowed Bear, running up the trail. "Wind, you been shootin' at some poor bird?"

"Look out, Bear," I screamed. "There's an Indian up here."

"What?" yelled Bear.

Then the Indian screamed out some Indian words, and Bear burst out laughing.

"Put down the gun," Bear shouted. "You like to scared him to death."

I turned to look at Bear, keeping the gun pointed at the Indian.

"Is he a friend?" I asked. "You sure? He held me by the throat with a knife."

"You let this little buck get away from you and nearly blow yer head off?" asked Bear, laughing.

"He like lizard," the Indian said. "Slippery as fish."

"Wind," said Bear. "Meet my brother Tall Elk, great warrior of the Crow nation."

Bear took me over and shoved me at the man.

"Tall Elk," Bear then said. "This is my white brother, Wind."

Tall Elk reached over and grabbed me. He took me in those iron fists of his and held me up to the sky. He turned me a couple of directions, looked at my teeth, and then embraced me.

"You be brother to Tall Elk, too, Wind," he said to me.

"I would be a brother to you," I told him.

Tall Elk screamed to the sky. Then he turned and presented me with a small pouch bearing a design of a bird-like person.

I took it and ran my hand along the fine workmanship. Then I went inside the cabin and brought out a fine beaver pelt I'd just finished working. I handed it to him.

"You make proud gift," Tall Elk told me. "You be fine brother to Crow."

We walked inside the cabin together with Bear. There was a warm fire in the fireplace, and we huddled around it. We were silent for a few minutes. Then Bear spoke something to Tall Elk in Crow words. The tall warrior looked upon Bear with sad eyes and answered his question. He told Bear other things, last of all showing his left hand, where two of his fingers had been cut off.

I remembered what the soldiers had told me about the Crows at the fort. They cut off fingers to mourn relatives. It came to me that something had happened to Bear's family. I searched Bear's eyes for tears. There were none.

I felt a tremble run through Bear's body, but it passed. Then he went on talking to Tall Elk about other things. When they finished, Bear opened an old chest in the corner of the cabin and took six jugs from it. They were of a kind Isaac had gotten in Independence and were filled with strong spirits. Bear took them all with him, disappearing outside the cabin.

Tall Elk followed, and I ran after both of them.

"What's wrong, Bear?" I shouted. "Tell me."

Bear turned for a moment and looked at me. His eyes were filled with sadness, but I saw there were no words for it. He took the jugs into the skin shed and closed the door. Tall Elk followed him, barring the door.

"Why did you do that?" I asked him. "He can't get out. I'm going in there."

"No," Tall Elk shouted, throwing me away from the shed. "Must be so," he said, blocking the way.

"I'm his friend," I said. "I can help him."

"Not now, my brother. You come with me. I try explain," Tall Elk said, taking my hand with a gentleness I'd not known since my mother died.

He didn't take me back to the cabin. Instead, he led me to the side of the mountain. There, looking out on the valley, he sat down.

"There is time when man must cry in silence," he told me.

"That doesn't make sense," I said. "How can a man cry in silence?"

"Does not cry with tears," he said. "Cries with heart," he explained, crossing his wrists and grinding them against each other to show me the pain.

"I know those kind of tears," I said.

"Is good," Tall Elk said. "You help Bear. He need you soon."

"What happened?" I asked.

"Sioux come. They fill valley of Big Horn. Many die. My sister die. Spring Antelope die."

"Bear's wife and son?"

"Boy was tall as bow. Next year, he come to Bear as Crow warrior."

"Was he as old as I am?" I asked.

"He have thirteen summers. Much taller."

"What will Bear do? Will he cut off his fingers?" I asked.

"Not know. Bear sad man. No tears in eyes. No love in hands. All in heart."

"He doesn't show it, but he loved them very much."

"He love. He love you, too."

"I don't think so," I said. "He likes me some. I'm company. That's all."

"You read hands, not heart. There fire in heart for you. He man of mountain. He brother to bear. He not give you sign with hands. Give you sign with heart."

I thought about the times he put his coat around me on cold nights. I thought about him going off alone against the grizzly. I thought about the hundred little things he did for me.

"I love him," I said. "Is it a manly thing to do?"

"You love father?" Tall Elk asked.

"My parents are dead."

"He be father to you. True?" he asked, gesturing with his hand straight out from his lips.

"Yes," I said. "True."

"Love good," Tall Elk told me. "Binds man and boy. You be son to Bear. He be father to you."

"I wish it were so," I said.

"Soon be," Tall Elk said. "Maybe words not come from Bear, but it be so."

"How long will he cry in silence?"

"Not long," he told me. "Then come hard times."

"Hard times?" I asked.

"Bear scream and fight. That why he lock away. Not want you see, me see. He do before. This last many day."

As I was about to ask him what would last many days, it began. Bear howled like nothing I'd ever heard before. He screamed so that I jumped. I was shaking, frightened, terrified.

"Is to be," said Tall Elk, grabbing my hand. "We be brothers to Bear. We let this thing be."

I began to understand. I had to endure this so that he could get over his grief. It was kind of like burying my nightmares.

"When can I go to him?" I asked.

"He must answer grief within own heart. You will know when."

We sat alone on the mountainside in silence. Then Tall Elk turned to me.

"Do you know Crow people?" he asked.

"No," I said. "I met some Crows from Ft. Laramie. And I've met you. I don't know the Crow people."

"I tell you great spirit legend. You listen?"

"Yes," I said, my eyes growing wide. "I'd love to hear a story."

"In time before man come, there was great before people. They tall, dark red. People fierce in battle. Fiercer than Crow or Sioux or Blackfoot. Kill all enemy."

"I see," I said.

"Before people believe they fall in battle. All die. They say of all warriors, last must go to tell others of their ways. They say last warrior must live life of lone eagle, search world for truth. Tell all men of ways of before people. Crow believe before people now powerful spirits. They say last warrior still walk."

Tall Elk swallowed deeply. Then he looked over the

valley as if he was searching for someone. Then he continued.

"Crow people believe greatest honor to be last warrior," he told me. "Never defeat last warrior. He go on. Before people give him life for all time."

"Why?" I asked.

"He sing songs of before people. He speak of great spirits. He tell of things to be."

"Do the Crows believe he's still alive?"

"Yes. Believe he walk valleys and sing songs. No man can see. Only pure in heart see sometime. Believe last warrior send great victory."

"I'd like to be the last warrior," I said. "I'd like to live forever and send victory to the brave."

"Not Tall Elk. Last warrior saddest of all spirits. He walk alone. Great warrior, but heart broken by people. No great warriors now. All good die. Brave hearts torn with pain."

"It's neat to think that he might be out there somewhere."

"Maybe you be great warrior," Tall Elk told me. "Maybe you see him."

"Have you ever seen him?" I asked.

"I hear him sing. I young. Great battle I in. Kill many Sioux and Cheyenne."

"What did he sing?" I asked.

"I sing for you," Tall Elk said, his eyes shining.

Tall Elk sang for me. The chant was haunting, ringing out through the valley with its ghostly tone. The words in Crow blended into each other, and Tall Elk's eyes burned fiercely. When he finished, he sank into the snow, exhausted.

"What do the words mean?" I asked. "I have to know."

"Song have no white man words. I give you some."

"I raise my voice to the heavens,
Summoning the spirits of the mountains.
I stand tall on the high ground
And look to the buffalo valleys below.
I walk with tall shoulders,
For my bow has the true aim.
My father is the storm cloud,
My mother, the summer rain.
I am kindred to the moon and the sun,
And my brother is the wind.
I see and know all men,
For I have walked among them.
There are the raven and the snake,
The deer and the elk and the bear.
I have seen their hearts, all,
Yet I walk alone among the whispering pines;
For I am the last warrior."

"The words are beautiful," I told him. "They speak to me."

"There is great sadness in the song. It is journey that never end."

"I'm like him," I whispered to myself. "I stand here and look out to the valleys. I've seen all kinds of men, yet I walk alone."

"You speak in silence," Tall Elk told me. "Yet your thoughts sing across the mountain. Be brave, but be not like last warrior. Be much. Be son to Bear. Use heart as well as bow arm."

"I'll try," I told him.

I wanted to be a son to Bear, but his days of suffering were only beginning. It was more than a week before silence filled the skin shed. Tall Elk went to open the door, but I outran him. I found Bear on the floor, surrounded by the empty jugs. He'd not eaten all that time, and he was weak.

I tried to carry him, but it was not possible. Tall Elk and I together got him into the cabin and warmed him. I got him to eat some broth, and the next morning he was himself again.

"Was I unmanly?" he asked me when Tall Elk went outside.

"You were grieving for your family," I said.

"He tell you?"

"Yes," I said. "He told me much. He told me about the last warrior and about my brothers, the Crow."

"I have shamed myself," Bear said, looking away from me.

"No," I said. "You have opened your heart for once. Look, Bear, I found out something. When you were hurting in that shed, I wanted to go to you."

"Why?" he asked.

"Because I care about you. Because I care about you. Because . . . because I love you, Bear."

I tried to wipe the tears from my eyes. It wasn't possible, though. I was only nine in spite of myself, and I'd been a man too much that week. I went to him and plunged my face into his great hairy shoulder.

"Stop that, Wind," he told me.

"I can't," I told him. "I can't be like that warrior. I need you."

"It's all right," he said, lifting me to his knee. "I understand."

I looked up at him, seeing a new warmth in his eyes. I hugged him with all the strength that my small arms could manage.

"It'll be better from now on," Bear told me. "You be a kid when you need to be. Maybe, . . ." he said, pausing, "maybe you can learn to be a kid again."

"And you?" I asked him.

"Maybe I can be a father to you."

X

Tall Elk left us later that month. It seemed strange to me that I should be without his wisdom and stories. He had brought me to Bear and Bear to me, though, and I knew he'd left us richer for his having come our way.

The winter snows fell and fell. Bear told me he'd never had a winter with so much snow. The Indians that roamed through the valley in hunting parties vanished. Only the strongest herds of animals—the elk, large deer and some moose—continued to roam the Tetons.

It was a wonderland to me. Dressed warmly, I made a sled of pine planks and roared down a nearby rise on our mountain. I screamed and tumbled and nearly buried myself with that sled, but it brought a smile from Bear. I was being nine again, and it brought him pleasure.

The sledding came to a halt soon, though. One morning we woke to discover we were totally snowbound. Only our wood and food supply inside the cabin could serve us now. The snow drifts blocked the great door and were nearly as high as the windows.

It was hopeless for Bear to try to get out a window, and I could not free the door by myself. Instead, I squirmed out the windows each morning and kept them free. When necessary, I got some needed item from the skin shed or checked the traps near the cabin. I also made sure the horses and mules were fed.

When I finished my duties, I'd return to the cabin and Bear would tell me stories. For two days, we did nothing else. But he grew tired of the telling, and I could see him growing restless. I went through my things and saw what I'd almost forgotten. My books.

There were a number of them, but some I'd already read. The knights of the round table seemed out of place. But there was one book my mother had always considered her favorite. It was written by a man named Cooper, who lived in New York. It was called *The Last of the Mohicans*, and was about Indians.

I took it in my hand and walked over to Bear.

"Bear," I said, "would you like to read?"

"Cain't," he said. "My pa wasn't much up on kids goin' to school. Waste o' time, he always said."

"Oh," I sighed, "would you mind if I read to you, then?"

"That'd be nice, Wind," he told me. "Always wondered what was in those books o' yer ma's."

I started in with Mr. Cooper's book. It was about some Englishmen and some Frenchmen before our country got started. It was mostly in favor of the Englishmen and the Mohican Indians. The head Frenchman, Montcalm, was a real scoundrel, allowing the English to surrender, then slaughtering a bunch of them. Bear didn't much like him either.

I would read part of the book, and then we'd talk awhile.

"That fellow who wrote down all that didn't know Indians much," Bear told me one time. "Indians don't act so much like white men."

"They were eastern Indians," I told him. "It was a long time ago."

"Pretty stupid Indian to get himself killed for a white woman. Most Indians wouldn't've given up no captive, either."

"It's just a story," I told him.

"If a guy's goin' to take the trouble to write some things down in a book, he might as well git it right."

"They're different Indians, Bear," I told him.

We got to a point where Bear just couldn't put up with Mr. Cooper anymore. I liked the book, especially Uncas. He was the young Indian who was loyal to his white friend, Hawkeye. When Uncas died, I cried a little. That really made Bear mad.

"Book ain't supposed to make kids cry," he yelled, throwing the book across the room.

I had to finish the last bit by myself. When I finished it, I went through the books that were left until I found something he didn't know about. There was a bright green book that Helen got me from a schoolmaster. It was called *Oliver Twist*, and was written by a man from England.

It turned out to be a success with us. It was about a little English orphan who had a rough time. Bear didn't like how they treated Oliver, and neither did I. Since Bear didn't know about London, he figured Mr. Dickens, who wrote the book, was probably all right.

"I believe I'd belted that old guy, too," Bear said after Oliver had attacked a big kid for saying something not at all nice about his mother. "I'd really belted that'un."

"Bear, he'd never have said it to you. Oliver's more like me. He's just a little kid. He's an orphan, too. Just like me."

"I's an orphan, you know," Bear told me.

"You never told me that," I said. "Your folks died?"

"Ma died when I was thirteen," he said, pausing. I could see that made him think of his son, and he tried to get over it.

"What happened to your pa?" I asked.

"Pa was no 'count. He was drunk most o' the time. Beat Ma the rest o' the time. I got my brothers, Henry and John, to my Aunt Mary. Then I went back to settle with Pa."

"How'd you settle?" I asked him.

"I was fifteen, but bigger than he was by half a foot. I stove the side o' his head in."

"You killed your own father?" I asked.

"Surprised you, didn't I?" asked Bear. "They still probably wants me fer murder back in Indiana."

"If you killed him, there must have been a reason," I said.

"He was cruel, heartless," Bear said. "He'd tell us how he cared fer us. Then he'd beat us an' lie to us an' leave us hungry. He weren't no pa at all."

"Did he hit you that night?" I asked.

"Four or five times."

"How many times did you hit him?"

"Jest once." Bear frowned. "Wind, I really wish I hadn't hit that man. He was cruel, and he worked an' beat Ma right to death. But he was my pa, and I wish I hadn't done it."

"I know," I said.

"Anyhow, I left home then. I was fifteen, but big fer my age. I worked my way down the river to St. Louis. I settled there awhile. Had a nice little gal fer a wife an' a pretty little baby boy. They died one winter, though, so I headed West."

Bear paused a moment, swallowing a tear. Then he went on.

"I hopped a freight to Independence. It was '43, an' the first wagons to California were rollin'. I got a job workin' stock, an' I made it all the way to Sacramento. On the way back, I found the Tetons, an' they found me. Been here since."

"It's tough being all alone," I said. "I wonder sometimes about my brothers and sister. I've got some nieces and nephews, too, you know."

"Might have some myself," Bear said. "I wrote a letter —well, got one written fer me—to Aunt Mary from St. Louis. I jest wanted them to know why. I never tried to git in touch with 'em again. Wouldn't do nobody no good."

"Don't you wonder what they look like?" I asked him. "Don't you wonder what they like to do? Don't you want to see them?"

"Nope," said Bear. "I got this mountain. It's a good life, better'n most. Now I got you, Wind, fer company. It's 'nough."

"I wonder about my brothers and my nieces and nephews. I wonder if Helen's little girls will be as pretty as she is. I wonder if they all love me still."

"Somethin' else, too, ain't there?" Bear asked me.

My eyes could never hide anything from him. I swallowed and turned to face him.

"They must think I'm dead."

"You'd like to send 'em word?"

"Yes," I said. "But that would end me staying here, wouldn't it?"

"Wind, you can stay here as long as you like," he told me. "Every year I meet th'other trappers at the rendezvous. We meet with the Hudson Bay Company people. They buy our goods, an' we swap the money fer ammunition, new rifles, store goods, knives and such. Used to spend the rest on a good time. Might be able to get you somethin'. Might be able to send off a letter."

"If I didn't tell them where I was, it'd be all right, wouldn't it?"

"Sure, Wind," he said. "Sure."

We finished *Oliver Twist* before the snows thawed. I also finished my letter, writing it in my rough hand with a stick from the fire. Matthew had told me that was how Abe Lincoln wrote his lessons. It probably worked better for him than for me, though.

When the snows melted, Bear prepared to make the rendezvous. They called it Pierre's rendezvous, after an old half-Indian trapper. It was pretty wild, according to Bear, and he suggested I stay at the cabin. There would be plenty of fishing with the coming of spring, and I knew that if I was going to send my letter, I'd best stay out of sight. Martha might send word to the army to find me, and I wasn't ready to leave my new home.

One bright morning Bear rode off. He had the mules and even little Sunrise laden with furs and hides. I was eager to see what he'd bring back.

The days I was to spend alone would be long and difficult. It was about a thirty-mile trip through the mountains to Pierre's Hole. Bear would be gone about two weeks. I went out that first day and shot at some birds. Then one of them tumbled from the sky, and I walked to where its blood stained the snow.

I realized it was for nothing. The bird wasn't big enough to eat. I hated myself for killing it just for fun. I put the gun aside and spent the rest of the day fishing.

The second day Bear was gone, I felt something behind me. It was like a shadow falling over me, and I slowly pulled my trusty Colt from my belt. Flipping over suddenly, I pointed the gun at the intruder, who was none other than Bear.

"Mighty short rendezvous," I said, smiling, glad to have him back.

"Mighty lucky." Bear smiled back at me. "I almost got my fool head blown off. After what happened to Tall Elk, I oughta know better'n to surprise you."

"What happened at the rendezvous?" I asked.

"Met up with an old friend named Maurice. He's half-Flathead Indian. He traps to the north o' us. He's headed for the rendezvous, so I made a deal with him. He'll take our goods down, mail yer letter, and bring back the supplies."

"But you wanted to go yourself."

"Rather be 'round here, Wind," he told me. "You never spent a spring in the mountains."

"I would have been all right," I said. "We'll likely get taken on the furs."

"Nope. Hudson man knows me. He cheats me, he knows I'll find him. He knows Bear."

"It would have given you a chance to get drunk and have a good time. I'd have been all right."

"Can have a good time here," he said, sitting down beside me. "There's things I got to tell you 'bout spring."

"Like what?" I asked.

"Like them Sioux that comes through here sometimes on their way to the Yellowstone. If they don't, the Gros Ventre and Blackfeet likely will. Then there's the Nez Perce."

"I could stay out of their way," I said.

"Don't want you to. Want you to learn who they is and what they is. You got to start knowin' how to talk to 'em. Might save yer hide, not to mention yer pretty yellow hair."

I hadn't cut my hair in a long time, and it was long and flowing. It might be pretty tempting for some wild buck to add to his collection.

"Teach me the ways of the mountains," I told him.

"We'll start with trackin'," he told me.

Leading the way down the mountain, my thirst for knowledge and adventure overwhelmed both of us. It would be an exciting spring, a learning spring. I would be a mountain man by next winter.

XI

Five winters passed under the western sky, and in their passing I learned many things. My eyes now saw things they never noticed before. I could feel in my bones a deer, an elk or a Sioux now long before I could see it.

Now I walked the mountains and valleys with new knowledge. I could speak the tongue of the Crow, the Cheyenne and the Shoshoni. I knew the seasons, and I could read the weather in the clouds.

I was now fourteen years old, or would have been that age in Ohio. I'd not grown tall in the mountains, but I was less of a boy now. Bear always said he was born in the beginning, before the world began. I felt that way myself now. It was as if time had no place in the mountains. Everything there was ageless. Man or beast, it mattered not how old but how strong and how clever.

I worried about my strength, but not my cunning. I had a great teacher, and I knew the ways of my enemies. I was not big yet, only slightly over five feet in height. But my legs ran with the wind, and I was quick as a deer.

My shoulders always seemed too frail to me. My face was thin, like my mother's, and it appeared I'd never grow dark and sour like Bear. But there was a broadening in my shoulders, a lengthening in my legs, and my arms grew taut as a bow string ready for battle.

I'd spent five winters in the Tetons, and for five springs I'd followed Bear through the valleys. I was at home along the great rivers or among the great peaks. In our wanderings, we had hunted and fished the Snake, the Yellowstone, the Wind, the Big Horn, and even the mighty Missouri.

I'd seen Indians of a hundred tribes. Some, like the Crow and the Arikara, I felt like a brother to. Others, like the Cheyenne and the Sioux, I knew would never ride into my sight without bringing danger.

With the coming of spring, our pelts had been sent off again to the rendezvous. When old Maurice returned with our goods, I knew it would be his last spring. There is a mark of death in the mountains, and it was upon our old friend. We never saw him again.

Bear had news for me I didn't wish to hear. Our brothers the Crow had fled the Big Horn and the buffalo valleys to the west of there.

There were Sioux there now, and we would not hunt it this year. I loved the Yellowstone and the Big Horn best of all the rivers, for there was a freshness in the land there.

Instead, we would journey to the south and hunt the Snake. The Snake was a dangerous river there. The tribes that used to camp beside the river were peaceful, but lately we had seen Cheyenne there. The Teton Sioux also camped there. They were allied with the Cheyenne, and we were always careful when we were around them.

The Snake was a bold river, cutting its way through rock two mountains high. That part of the river was good for fishing and hunting, but one had to keep an eye open for the weather. A flood could carry a man or a village away in an hour.

We rode through the valley with eyes full of caution. There was no sign of danger, and that brought fear to us. This was a land of enemies, and their absence in one place only meant their presence in another.

"The Teton Sioux've taken their lodges elsewhere," Bear told me as we rode through one of their camps. "I've been through this valley a hundred times, but never without meeting at least women and children at this place. It's a spirit place for 'em, the burial place of a great chief. There is danger in its emptiness."

"Where would they go?" I asked.

"There've been no soldiers. Ain't sure what's happenin'. Cain't be good, though."

We slept in a cave, keeping our guns armed and ready. There was a strangeness everywhere, and I felt uneasy. When we reached the great bend in the Snake, we'd still seen no Indians. Worse, the valleys were filled with buffalo, and it was not right for buffalo to be far from hunting parties.

We busied ourselves with our fishing. Then we set out our traps. There was also a fine day of buffalo hunting. For the first time, I killed a bull buffalo with the huge buffalo gun. My shoulder stung for days, but there were no blotches of blue, and it had not bled.

I looked with pride at my reflection in the river. I had still not grown within a foot of Bear's height, but my shoulders, though slim, were firm and solid. And there was a feel of leather to my skin.

Each afternoon I swam in the Snake. Bear had grown

less fond of water than ever, and he'd use it only when I insisted he bathe. He'd picked up the habit from me in the first place, and if not for my jests about his smell, he'd never have ventured so much as a toe in the river. I swam for the joy of it, just as I ran for the feel of the wind across my face.

We camped along the Snake almost a week before I felt one day that eyes were on my back. I was taking my afternoon swim, and my rifle was lying with my clothes on the river bank. I saw it with my eyes, but I still felt the cold stare of other eyes on my back. I waded slowly back to the bank and the security my rifle would bring. Then I turned around to face my visitor.

When I saw him, I almost laughed out loud. He was a boy, thin like myself. He wore the markings of the Cheyenne, though, and my memory told me he was not to be taken lightly. In his tribe, he was already a man.

I watched him with eyes full of suspicion. There was a clear gleam in his eyes, but he did not look to be in search of battle. At last, he held out his hand in peace. I matched his gesture.

A broad smile came to his lips, and he stripped his shirt and leggings from his thin body. One could tell he was not well fed, and I wondered if the Cheyenne had seen the buffalo herd.

I called to him in Cheyenne that I came in friendship and would share my river with him.

He laughed at this, saying the rivers of the earth belong only to the greatest of the spirits, and that I was like the buffalo who grazes the prairie. I would soon leave behind me what was not mine.

There was wisdom in his words, and I smiled to him.

"You are Cheyenne," I told him in his own tongue, pointing from the sky to him in the way of his people.

"I am called Squirrel," he said. "I am son of Red Hawk, great war leader of the Cheyenne people."

"I am Wind," I said. "I am of the tall mountains. I dance among the clouds and laugh in thunder."

The Cheyenne boy moved backward.

"You have the hair of the sun, and there is sky in your eyes," he told me.

I saw he was afraid of me, not having seen anyone with blond hair and blue eyes before. At least he'd not seen one who could speak to him in his own tongue.

"Are you spirit or man?" he asked me.

"I am flesh as you are flesh," I told him. "But who's to say what spirit is?"

I knew he'd know that I was a man, but I added the last to leave him just a bit unsure.

"What tribe do you come of?" he asked. "Are you Gros Ventre or Blackfoot? Shoshoni or Nez Perce?"

"I am of the mountain," I told him. "I live with my brother, Bear, who is like the rock."

"I have heard of such a man," Squirrel told me. "It is said that he has killed the bear with his hands, and that he is now part spirit."

"It is so," I said. "I too have killed the bear, my first when I was but half a man."

I showed him the necklace of bear claws I always wore around my neck, even when the rest of me was bare. He tossed away the knife he wore on his hip and waded forward in the river. I set my rifle down and moved forward through the river to meet him.

Squirrel came close to me and set his hand upon the

necklace. His eyes grew wide, and he felt my skin to make sure that I was just a man.

"I will give to you a claw for your own luck, Squirrel," I told him. "It will bind us, one to the other. But tell me first why the great Cheyenne should come so far toward the setting sun."

"We come, my father and I, to take our brothers to the gathering. All Cheyenne go. Also Sioux, eastern and western tribes."

"Gros Ventre?" I asked.

"Some ride with us. Most have left their hunting grounds and moved to the south. They are cousins to the coward Crow, who ride with the white man to steal our lodges."

It somehow had failed to occur to Squirrel that I was a white man, and I was glad I didn't tell him I was a brother to the Crow.

"Here is your token," I said, handing him the claw from my necklace. "May it make your bow arm steady and your life thread strong."

"We are as brothers, you and I," he said. Then he ran through the river back to the bank. He took something from his clothes and splashed his way back to me.

"You will wear this badge of honor," he told me, handing me a bracelet that looked to be of silver. "It may save your life in the days to come. It is said that there is a long knife who comes to call his own death. This man is said to have yellow hair. If it is to be for him to die, then others will surely follow. It may be wise to wear this silver shield that you may live."

I clasped his strong arm, and he clasped mine. Then I felt the sun pass behind a cloud, and I knew it was time

for boys to be men. We left our separate ways, and I ran
to find Bear.

I told him what I had learned, and he stared at the sky
with his deep, thoughtful eyes.

"All ain't well here, Wind," he said. "Crows have a
sayin' for this. They say the sky is alive with thunder.
Lightning must surely follow."

"What does it mean, Bear?" I asked.

"Means Cheyenne and Sioux're goin' huntin'. For white
men. They aim to fight the army. Big war will follow. We
best be careful in the days ahead. Sleep lightly."

We kept no fire at night now. The spring was not yet
warm in the way of the Big Horn, and I shivered in my
sleep. One night a strange dream came to me. It was filled
with fire, and I saw Squirrel riding into battle with soldiers. There was a piercing cry from his throat. Then
blood filled his lips. I woke screaming.

"Stop that noise, Wind," Bear told me, covering my
mouth. "Yer goin' to wake the night. I ain't too eager to
find them Cheyenne."

"I had a dream," I said. "It was of a battle."

"You been talkin' to that Cheyenne buck too much.
He's got you all shook. You gotta get yer head back."

"There was fire in it, Bear," I said. "I never had a
dream with fire in it before. Yellow fire, red fire, orange
fire. The fire danced all around. Then Squirrel rode
through it all. There was a shot, and he died."

"You see who else was in the dream? Was we in
there?"

"No. A soldier shot him," I told Bear.

"Probably just dreamin'. He told you they was goin'
after some soldiers. You imagined the rest."

"But the fire made it so real," I said, clutching his arm. "You sure 'bout the fire?"

"Yes," I said. "I could feel its heat."

Bear reached his hand over and laid it across my forehead. He pulled it away, and for the first time, I read fear in his eyes.

"That Squirrel a friend o' yers?" he asked me.

"Not really," I answered. "I don't know him except for that day in the river."

"He's goin' to die in some battle. You saw it. Some spirit intended fer you to see it. I heard o' spirits talkin' 'fore, but never seen it. Scary."

"You think what I saw will happen?" I asked.

"I do." He frowned. "You remember anything else? Could mean somethin' to us."

"No," I said, frowning too. "I saw only the fire and the soldier shooting Squirrel."

"Did you know his face?" Bear asked. "The soldier's."

"I don't think so. He might have looked like one of the men at the fort, but I guess they're the only soldiers I've ever seen."

"Didn't look like you, though, did he?" Bear asked.

"No," I said. "He had a beard."

Bear sighed and sat up.

"Probably jest a nightmare," he said. "Still, I think we'll head north tomorrow. Don't like this river no more. There's a spirit here."

"It won't be angry?" I asked him.

"He sent you a warnin'," Bear said. "You didn't see 'nough to know what it was, but we'll be mighty careful fer a spell."

We spent the spring and summer in the Teton Valley.

There were no elk to hunt, but we went after a buffalo herd once. There were plenty of rabbits and several deer. The fishing was good, too. In late summer, the Gros Ventres returned, but we saw no Teton Sioux. There was still thunder in the skies, but with autumn on the wind, I had other worries.

XII

When we rode up to our mountain, we received a big surprise. A giant spruce tree had fallen on the cabin during the summer, and it was necessary to make repairs. At first it seemed that we could replace the roof and one side of the cabin. We soon realized, though, that the force of the tree had done too much damage. We used the walls of the first cabin as the foundation for a new one. Then we cut wood day and night to beat the first snows.

We won our race with the weather. Bear planned the new cabin, and with the two of us, it was soon completed. It was like a palace to me. We put a big storeroom in back, and there was more room than before. Bear lined the walls with heavy buffalo hides. It seemed far more a home than the old cabin.

The winter of my fifteenth year was actually a very mild one. The snows fell, but not enough to spoil our hunting. We had a rich beaver haul, and there were several beautiful foxes. I shot five deer, too, but my greatest adventure was an elk hunt.

Always before when we went after elk, Bear had insisted I ride behind him, shooting only if he missed his shot. He rarely did, so mostly my going along was for company. This time, though, we rode side by side. I knew this meant I would have my chance.

The great elk herd was grazing in a meadow when we found them. We were careful to approach them with the wind in our faces, keeping our scent hidden. We left the horses tied behind us, walking slowly and cautiously ever closer.

"Remember, Wind," Bear told me, "take yer aim and hold yer arm steady. Then squeeze the trigger."

I'd shot all kinds of game before, but always with my rifle. Now I cradled in my arms the great elk gun. It was heavy in my thin arms, but new power came from pride, and I held the gun steady.

"Wait," said Bear, his arm lightly moving the gun aside. "Come up an' see."

I snaked my way under the brush and lay beside him.

"Do you see him?" he asked me.

"The big one?" I asked back.

"The giant. He must be the father o' all elk. But watch th'other, too."

"The other?" I asked.

"Yes, Wind. There is always th'other. The younger."

"I see him," I said, watching a second giant elk approach.

"There'll be a challenge," Bear said. "Watch."

"They will fight? Why?" I asked.

"Who's to say fer sure? To see who's leader. Perhaps fer some sleek doe. Or fer the glory. Who's to say?"

"Perhaps," I said thoughtfully, "it's just the way of elk. There is a pride, perhaps, that makes it so."

"Look now," Bear whispered to me.

The great father elk advanced before the younger, dip-

ping his great antlers to the left. He scraped his right
forefoot against the snow. The younger drew back.

"The younger will charge," Bear told me.

I nodded my understanding.

The young elk repeated the elder's movements. Then
he charged. The old elk charged, too. They met with a
thunderous crash, the snow shaking from the trees.

"Shouldn't we shoot now?" I asked.

"It'd anger the spirits to kill them now."

I smiled at his words. They came of my own heart.

The young buck struck a second time at the old one.
Then a third. The old one spun and struck the younger.
There was thunder in the meadow. I found a feeling
within me, speaking to me. It made me a brother to the
old one, fighting back against the strength that must win.

"Why does he fight still?" I asked Bear. "He is the
weaker. Why not step back?"

"I's seen 'em before," Bear told me. "The young one
has the strength. The old one has the cunning. He may
still have his trick."

I watched closely, waiting for the old elk to strike. At
last he did, grinding his antlers hard against the younger.
There was a movement backward from the younger. The
old elk struck again, this time sending the younger back
hard. The third time, the old elk sent the younger back
into a tree.

There was a stillness in the air. The younger elk was
down, his great strong head splintered against the tree.
My heart leaped into my throat, but Bear's heavy hand
pulled me back to the ground.

"Look at the herd," Bear told me.

There was a stirring, and I thought that perhaps they

might have caught our scent. But it was something else. They saw what I had not. The great old father elk turned to face them, bearing only one antler. The other was broken.

In sadness, I watched a big buck step out from the herd. This second challenge was too much for me. The old one knew he must step aside, and I felt a great grief.

Bear looked to me as I raised the gun. I pointed the big gun at the new challenger, preparing to save the old one.

"You cain't kill 'em all," Bear told me. "It's the way o' the mountain. The strong'll live. The weak must die."

I nodded my head, a rare tear coming to my eye.

"He fought bravely," I said. "He should meet a better end."

"It's fer you to say," Bear told me.

"I understand what must be," I said. "I will do it."

I took the big elk gun and swung it around toward the old warrior. I fixed him in my sights and swallowed hard.

"I'll make your death quick and painless," I whispered to the elk.

As if he heard me, he turned his proud head to look at me. I saw he understood, and I checked the sights one last time. Then I shot him through the heart.

The blast of my shot started a stampede among the elk. The others scattered while I watched the great one fall. His blood stained the snow, and I walked toward him.

"I'm sorry I took your life," I told him. "It was as it had to be."

We took the two great elk, the victor and the loser, back to the cabin. Their hides hung on our wall, and we ate from their meat. It was a thing I did without joy, but it was a thing I'd grown to understand. It was life coming out of death. It was the way of the mountain.

I sat alone by the fire that night, and Bear noticed how I was different.

"Wind, you mourn this elk too much. It was his time," Bear told me.

"I know," I said. "But when will it be my time?"

"You shouldn't be too bothered with that," he said, laughing. "Yer still a boy."

"I'm growing," I said. "I can hold the elk gun steady. This past year I've outgrown two pairs of moccasins. In another month, I'll be able to shave."

"Takes more'n two hairs to shave," Bear said.

"There will be more," I said. "I may not be a big man, but I'm coming to be a man just the same. Does that not mean that I'm coming to my time?"

"Man don't choose his time," Bear told me. "Don't know it, neither. Man's time comes, it comes. When it comes, he likely feels it."

"How unfair life is," I shouted. "The old elk fought his greatest battle. He should have lived to celebrate his victory. He should have won something for his courage."

"He won a quick death," Bear said.

"What of Jerome? He fought bravely. He died slow and young. What about him?"

"Don't know," Bear sighed.

"And Bear," I said. "What of me? If Jerome died so young, what of me? Am I to die young, too?"

"Who's to say, Wind?" he asked. "Who's to say? I had two sons. One died 'fore he'd hardly lived. The Crow boy was not yet so tall as you when the Sioux killed him. Who's to say?"

The gloom that hung over my head became nothing to that which hung that winter over Bear. I should have known better than to have started talking about dying young. It had been six years since Bear's son had fallen to the Sioux, but the boy was never long forgotten. I had brought it back to him.

I felt the onset of spring in my bones, and an idea sprang forth. The rendezvous would arrive without Maurice this year. We would go together.

"Bear," I said to him one evening, "a great idea has come to me. We must lift our spirits. We will go to the rendezvous this year at Pierre's Hole."

Bear turned to face me.

"I'd 'most forgotten," he said. "Maurice woulda been here by now. I saw the sign o' his death on his face. I must go this year."

"It will lift your spirits," I said. "You can get drunk and get a woman, if you want."

"I's past the woman time o' my life," he said. "But there's things 'bout the rendezvous that sing to me of my youth."

"I've never seen it," I said to him. "Tell me what I need to know."

"You cain't go, Wind," he told me.

"Why?" I asked. "Why can't I? I'm old enough."

"Next year, Wind," he said. "You will go next year. This year you'll stay."

"But . . ."

"Trust me, Wind," he said. "I knows the signs o' the mountains. You gotta wait. There's strange things happenin' here, an' you'd best watch the cabin."

"I'll do as you say," I said. "I'll be all right here, so you needn't worry."

"I know that, Wind." He smiled, putting his great hairy hand on my shoulder. "I believe I might miss you a bit, though. I'll bring you somethin' back."

"Just bring yourself back," I told him.

"It's not my time yet," Bear said. "It'd take more'n there is out there to take ol' Bear."

We got the furs loaded and prepared food for his journey. It worried me that he was going all alone, but I knew that when he said something, it was more likely to be for my good than for his. I didn't argue with him as he rode off down the mountain.

I turned away from the path and walked back to the cabin. There was no warmth in the fire, and the cold grip of loneliness fell upon me. I watched the fire dance across the hearth, and I sang myself to sleep.

XIII

Bear had been gone only one day when I first felt something was wrong. There was a feeling in the back of my mind that something was about to happen. The hair on the back of my neck stood on edge, and I started dropping things.

I decided I'd better take a look around. I went to the animal shed and led Sunrise out. Sunrise was a bit worn, having been with me so long. But I trusted the little pony, and I had turned down repeated offers by Bear to trade him for a new horse.

There must have been something in the air, for Sunrise stomped his feet, then pawed the ground. He snorted at me, and nearly bit my hand when I put on his bridle. The horse never acted that way, and I grew concerned. When I got him saddled, I rode off to check the river.

I half expected to ride out into a Sioux war party, but the valley was empty. I turned next to check our traps on the river, but they were fine. I took one beaver and one rabbit from the traps. Then I headed Sunrise back up the mountain.

When I neared the cabin, I saw my first trace that something really was wrong. We'd placed some traps around a small spring. They were torn out of the ground, and there were traces of blood there.

I tied a jittery Sunrise to a pine tree. Then I went over to investigate. I didn't know what we had caught, but something had beaten me to the traps. I feared the worst, another bear. But it had been a smaller creature. I checked its tracks and saw that it was a large wolf.

"You tried to tell me, didn't you, Sunrise?" I told my horse. "I've never had dealings with a wolf before."

The horse whined nervously, and I went back to him. I heard a rustling in the brush and leaped on my horse just in time. The wolf bared her teeth at me, growling in defiance. I was scared half to death, and Sunrise was stomping the ground. The wolf made a run at me, but she had no stomach for a fight with a horse and withdrew. I got out my rifle, but Sunrise would not steady enough for me to get off a decent shot. My first round hit a tree, and the wolf disappeared into the underbrush.

I wheeled Sunrise around and headed back to the cabin. I unsaddled him and brushed his coat. He seemed to settle down after that, but I decided it was too dangerous to ride a nervous horse with the wolf around.

The next morning, I got a big surprise. There were wolf tracks all around the outside of the cabin. A strange feeling worked its way down my spine, and I had no appetite. It became clear to me that I could not wait for Bear to return. This wolf was on the attack. I had to kill her before she had her chance at me.

I'd never hunted a female creature, nor had I hunted a wolf. But there was much I had learned by myself on the mountain, and I knew this would have to be another.

I loaded my Colt revolver with six bullets. Then I took

the army rifle and cleaned it. I spent the rest of the day readying myself for the next morning. I didn't have the eyes of a cat, and I had no intention of hunting the wolf at night.

I slept little that night, though. I could hear my enemy prowling around the cabin, snarling at the door. There was a lump in my throat as I thought of the creature tearing at my flesh. I knew if the wolf got a good slash at me, I'd be finished.

I shook off a light slumber when the morning sun flashed through the cracks in the cabin windows. I was still tired, but there was a consciousness brought to me by fear.

I knew I had a battle ahead of me, just as the old elk had faced. The wolf was quicker and deadlier, but I was the smarter.

I ate a breakfast of dried venison and greens. What I didn't eat, I packed into a small leather bag. I also stuffed some extra ammunition and powder in the bag. I thought about leaving a note for Bear, but I remembered he couldn't read. The things I had to say were not for strangers' eyes, and he would know what had happened anyway.

It was warm enough outside for me to have gone bare, but I slipped my great bearskin coat over my shoulders. I also wore my Cheyenne bracelet. I tried to think of something else to do, but there was nothing. I knew my heart was ready for its trial, so I set out.

The trail of the wolf was fresh, and it gave my trained eyes no difficulty in following it. I walked with the rifle balanced lightly in my hands. I kept my pistol in my belt, uncocked. I preferred to leave the death of me to the wolf, and not let some unseen branch or hole in the ground do its work for it.

I'd never considered it before, but I would not be easy to kill. I was stronger than I seemed, even to myself. I was also quick on my feet.

I walked barefooted through the forest, quiet as the hawk circling its prey. Not even a whisper left my lips. My ears were open to every sound, and my eyes swept the ground in front of me for the slightest sign of danger.

I threaded my way through the brush, over the rocks and through two streams. Still my eyes caught the trail, and I swept through some high grass near the spring. At last my ears caught the sound of a whine. It was a cry unknown to my ears.

I followed the sound around a pile of boulders to a small cave. The whining noises came from that same cave. I knew at last what the sound was. Wolf cubs. I had been prepared for danger, but when I heard a deep growl from the cave, I knew I faced an enemy fiercer than any bear. A she-wolf guarding her den.

There was no question of me advancing into the cave. I had no night sight, and the wolf would be upon me in a second. My only chance was to wait outside and hope she would come out. If luck was smiling on me, she would come out in the light. If not, then I would have to return to the cabin, and the wolf would have her chance.

I waited until the sun was nearly behind the mountain to leave. I knew this wolf was not without cunning of her own. She knew I dared not face her in the night, and I could hear her following me in the fading light of dusk. I kept my gun ready, but she appeared in my view only once. I fired a single shot at her head, ripping off a branch. She vanished into the brush, and I reached the cabin safely.

Again that night the wolf prowled outside the cabin. I felt confined, trapped by this creature. Our game was a strange one. By day, I waited for her, ready to kill. By night, she waited for me, ready to do no less.

When daybreak came, I got my guns and prepared to seek her out again. This time my approach did not go unseen. I could feel her cold eyes on me all the way. I fired once in her direction, but it is difficult to hit what you can't see.

By the time I arrived at the cave, I could hear her growl deep within the rock. I waited the entire day for her to come out, but it wasn't to be. She followed my steps back to the cabin again that night, and I determined I must kill her.

"Creature of the night," I yelled to her, "I will kill you. You are brave and wise and cruel and strong, but I will kill you. For I must live, even if you must die."

There was a stillness in the air, as if the wolf paused to listen. Then there was a growl like I had never heard. It split the air and froze my spirit. But there was the thing to be done, and I ignored her noise. I lay down on the blanket as usual and found sleep.

The next morning, I awoke fresh. I knew somehow that it was to be the day of my test, and I struck out early. The wolf must die, and I knew how to see it done.

"How stupid I have been," I told myself. "I am the man here, and this wolf is but a beast. Yet it is she who has been thinking. I have the gift of wisdom, and it is with it that I must win my battles."

Several times I caught a glimpse of the wolf. Each time, though, she vanished before I could raise my rifle. When I reached the cave, I heard again her growl from within.

"Good, creature of the night," I shouted, "you are in a prison of your own design."

I then gathered wood and stacked it near the entrance of the cave. Each time I drew near, the wolf growled. But she was preparing for my entry, and not for my plan. When the woodpile was big enough, I set it alight.

The fire danced in the wind, and the flames bore inward toward the cave. I heard a great howl. Then there was great silence. As the flames burned on toward afternoon, I realized that all this while the smoke had gone inward.

"Fool!" I told myself. "There is a draft."

I knew there was a second opening to the cave. I realized I might have been killed had the wolf circled to strike me from behind. The light of day was fading, but I knew this was the day it must be done. I struck out for the other side of the hill, leaving the fire to seal the front.

Crossing the hill, I heard again the whine of the cubs. Then I saw them. There were three in all, none very old. I also saw their mother. The wolves were thin. I knew, of course, that they'd not have raided my traps had they been well fed. I understood my enemy, but I remembered something Bear had told me once.

"In such things there is no room for the heart," he'd said. "You must kill, for it is yer nature. The strong walk the mountain. The weak lie with their bones bleached white by the summer sun."

My heart trembled as I raised the rifle. The she-wolf

was nursing her cubs. I lined the sights on the mother, thinking to spare the children. But there was no sense in it, for the cubs could not live without their mother. This I knew already.

I fired the gun, and there was a great whelp. One of the cubs had moved, and my shot pierced the tiny body. The she-wolf raised her eyes to meet me, growling with my death chant on her lips. I could feel our life forces clashing.

She had a strong will to live. She knew her cubs must die with her. I had a strong will, too. I felt a love for life she could not understand. There were things left to be done with my life, and so I must live.

The wolf rushed toward me, but I held my fire. I waited for her to reach a rise of ground, and then I fired. The shot pierced the air, throwing the wolf backward. She landed near my feet, and I saw her die.

I watched the cubs come to her, whining in their ignorance. They wished to be nursed, but their mother was no more. I drew out my pistol and looked into their trusting eyes. They knew not why they were to die, nor did I. It was the mountain's way, and I did not wish them to die slowly of starvation, or serve as a dinner for some creature of the air.

I killed them for their mother's sake. Then I skinned the mother and buried them all in a pit. I would not have the birds eat their flesh. I prepared the wolf's hide. It would hang on the wall when Bear returned.

All kinds of thoughts rushed through my head that night. I could not bear to be at the cabin, so I saddled Sunrise and rode him out to the valley. I found a strangeness about me when I reached the top of the mountain. I tied my horse to a tree and sat down.

The day was bright, but I felt darkness about me. There was something moving across the valley in front of me. I saw, and yet I did not see. Perhaps it was only a specter. Maybe it was the spirit of the wolf. No, it was not a creature. It was a man.

What I saw was like a wisp of smoke riding toward me. But there were eyes which took me in their gaze, and I grew cold in their sight. Then a song fell upon my ears. It was familiar to me.

> I raise my voice to the heavens,
> Summoning the spirits of the mountains.
> I stand tall on the high ground
> And look to the buffalo valleys below.
> I walk with tall shoulders,
> For my bow has the true aim.
> My father is the storm cloud,
> My mother, the summer rain.
> I am kindred to the moon and the sun,
> And my brother is the wind.
> I see and know all men,
> For I have walked among them.
> There are the raven and the snake,
> The deer and the elk and the bear.
> I have seen their hearts, all,
> Yet I walk alone among the whispering pines;
> For I am the last warrior.

"I am Wind," I heard myself whisper. "I am a white

man. I was born in Ohio, and my parents are dead. I kill only out of need. I do not wish to fight."

I felt the stirring of the wind. My hair fell away from my face, swept back by the breeze. It was as if my mother was still alive. She had swept it back from my forehead in the same way when I was little.

"If you have words for me, spirit, speak to me," I called out to the valley below me. "I would not walk alone the world as you do. I would be with my brother, Bear."

I felt something touch me, not from the outside, but from within. My flesh grew cold, and Sunrise danced upon his feet. He flew up into the air, broke loose, and ran out into the valley.

I wanted to shout and run after him, but I found my feet frozen. Lightning lit the sky, and terror fell upon my brow. I was frightened, yet I could not run. I knew that there was nothing there but myself now, but there was a feeling. There was something. But the sky flashed clear before my eyes, and whatever was with me went away. When I finally got back to the cabin, Sunrise was waiting.

XIV

The spirit of the valley visited my dreams nightly. I found his ghostly arm reaching out for my hand. His eyes were fixed on mine, and I heard his haunting song roll all around me. His fingers touched me, and I woke up screaming.

"No!" I screamed out into the night. "If you are the last warrior, go on your way. I'll not go with you. I have my life here to live."

My head would clear, and I would realize it was only a dream.

"If Bear was here," I told myself, "this dream would go away. It's only because I have no one to tell of my courage. I'm lonely, and my head has taken to dreaming."

But it was more than that, no matter what I told myself. There was a feeling on the mountainside, and Sunrise would run off whenever I got him close to the river.

"Spirit," I would tell it, "if you are a spirit, leave me in peace. I've lost all I've ever had except my own life and my friend, Bear. Leave me alone with what I have."

Still the dreams came, and I tossed and turned in the way of the boy I was no longer. I saw the face of the spirit when I looked at the moon. There was a chill upon my spine even in the heat of midday.

I longed for the return of Bear. He would have words for all my troubles. He always did. I pained to hear those words. There must be something I could do. Perhaps I'd not performed some ceremony.

Then I began to worry about Bear. Perhaps something had happened to him. Maybe he'd found a Sioux war party. Perhaps there'd been a wolf where he was, too. Worse, I began to doubt his loyalty. What if I'd been left behind? What if he'd ridden off to another mountain? What if he'd left me to the spirit of the last warrior?

But it was all in my mind. Almost a week to the day after I'd shot the wolf, Bear's voice boomed across the mountain.

"Wind, I am home!" he shouted. "I've seen the valleys and I've seen the painted women. I've touched the clouds and I've walked the earth. No mountain can still my spirit, for I am home."

I ran down to greet him, jumping up behind him on the horse and casting my smile upon him.

"This horse o' mine might be laden already just with me, Wind," Bear told me. "He's a new one, and I'd hate to lose him."

I scrambled down and looked up at him. I wanted to reach out and hug him the way I had when I was little. But I was a man now, and Bear had never much cared for the touching, anyway. I just smiled.

"I believe you've grown," Bear told me. "There's a shine to you, too. You've had no trouble?"

"Not to speak of," I told him. "I'll tell you about it."

"We've had a great fortune from the furs," Bear told

me. "Weren't many trappers this year. Cheyenne an' Sioux've been scalpin' a lot o' white men. Got two bags o' gold. Only drank and womaned one o' them away."

"I thought you were past the age for women," I said.

"Well, I'll tell you, Wind," he said, a deep shine coming to his eyes. "There was a little gal from Canada. Her papa was a soldier. She was small an' light on her feet, an' it came to me that I'd be pleased with her. I was."

"Is your mind clear now?" I asked him.

"Yup," he said. "There was wisdom in you, Wind. Told me to go, an' you was right. I've buried the spirit o' my boy."

"Then let's go to the cabin," I said, leading the mules up the last rise.

We put away his great new horse and fed the mules. Three of the four were new and younger.

"What happened to old Horse?" I asked.

"He grew to be too old," Bear told me. "I got over the Tetons, but he was broken in spirit. He lay down, an' I gave him his end. He was a good beast."

"You bought this new one then?"

"An' three new mules. One o' the mules was still strong. Th'other two was gettin' old. The fourth I rode to the rendezvous, an' I traded it 'cause I grew to dislike its personality."

I laughed. I remembered riding a mule. It wasn't like riding a horse at all.

"We've talked enough out here," Bear said. "Come, let's go inside an' have some food. I's hungry from my journey, an' you's grown thin from my absence. We've much to say."

I followed him inside and readied some berries. Then I

took three trout from the cooling pool by our spring and cleaned them.

"Trout'll taste good," Bear told me. "I been eatin' buffalo steak fer a week."

"I caught these fresh this morning," I said.

Bear turned around and froze in his tracks. His eyes were locked on the wolf pelt, and he turned toward me.

"Where'd this come from?" he asked.

"It's a wolf's hide," I answered. "It came from a wolf."

"Any fool knows that much," he told me. "How'd you come by it?"

"After you left, a she-wolf came to the mountain. She raided our traps, and I set out after her."

"You set out after a she-wolf?" he asked. "Alone?"

"Yes, Bear," I said. "She attacked me by the traps, but I was able to dodge her. I fired at her, and she ran away."

"Go on," he said.

"I thought to go after her then, but when I saw she'd found the cabin . . ."

"She followed you to the cabin?" he asked. "Never heard o' no wolf doin' that."

"I found her tracks all over, so I set out to kill her."

"Tell me," he said.

"I followed her signs to a cave. I could hear her growls from inside, and then the whine of cubs."

"That's much danger," Bear said. "A she-wolf in her den is no easy thing. You didn't go in after her?"

"No, I waited outside. The sun went behind the mountain, though, and I went back to the cabin. She followed, and I slept little that night."

"You were glad of the cabin?"

"Yes," I said. "I was glad we built it strong. The day

after that, I did just the same. I waited for her by day, and she waited for me by night."

"This went on?" he asked.

"Another day. Then I knew that I must kill her. I built a fire at the mouth of the cave and waited for her to come out."

"You got her with the fire?"

"No," I said, smiling. "She was too clever, and I was too stupid. I watched the fire burn half the day before I realized it was smoking inside the cave."

"There was a draft," Bear said.

"Yes," I said. "Another entrance. I walked across the rocks and found it. The wolf was nursing her young, and I sorrowed. I didn't wish to kill a mother."

"It speaks well fer you," Bear said. "Takes great courage to do what must be done when yer heart ain't in it."

"I shot true, but a cub moved and caught the shell instead. The she-wolf charged me, and I remembered what you told me. Wait until it's for certain. Then I fired, and the wolf fell at my feet."

"What of the cubs?" Bear asked.

"I watched them come to her," I told him. "Tears clouded my eyes, but I would not have them fall prey to a hawk or a cat. I shot them, too. I skinned the mother and buried them all."

"It's well," he said, slapping his great hands down on my shoulder. "You've proven yer manhood. You've done a great thing."

That night I went to sleep with ease, hoping the warrior spirit would leave now Bear had returned. But the shadow of the spirit crossed my dreams again, and I woke screaming.

"Wind, wake up," Bear told me, shaking me.

"I am awake," I said. "He touched me again. This time I could feel him grasp my hand."

"Who touched you?" he asked. "What is it that shakes yer heart and walks yer dreams?"

"The last warrior," I said. "I saw him. I heard his song. I had just killed the wolf. I rode Sunrise out to the mountainside, but I felt strange. I got off the horse and sat down. Something seemed to be in the valley, and I felt uneasy. Sunrise went crazy, broke away, and ran off."

"Tell me the rest."

"I looked closely to see what it was. It wasn't anything I could really see, just a mist or cloud. But it was in the shape of a person, and I thought it might be an Indian. But it had no being. There was only smoke."

"You seen it before?" he asked.

"Never."

"What did you hear?"

"His song. It was the same as Tall Elk sang, except he sang it to me in English. It was beautiful, but there was a tone to it that froze my heart. It frightened me. I felt him coming for me."

"You didn't wish to go with him?" Bear asked.

"No," I said. "I told him I wished to stay with you. I didn't want to be alone like him. My place was with you, not roaming the mountains all alone."

"Then what?"

"He touched me. It wasn't like the touch of a man, but like a cold piece of cloth falling on my shoulder. It frightened me, and I ran from him."

"Now he walks yer dreams?"

"Yes," I said. "I must have done something wrong. Perhaps killing the wolf?"

"No," Bear said. "I have heard Tall Elk tell o' this spirit. It's th'one that frightens man most. Death we must all face. Life alone ain't the same. Tall Elk told me this spirit stalked him for a full moon after he fought a battle."

"Did he go away then?" I asked.

"Yes," Bear told me. "But Tall Elk told me the spirit will return some day to ask again. Tall Elk believes this to be great medicine. One day he will go off with the spirit. You, too, if it is so, will have a choice again."

"I don't know about all that," I said. "Couldn't it just be a dream? Couldn't it just be because I'm afraid?"

"Sure it could be," he said. "But were you afraid o' the wolf? Were you afraid o' the bear you shot? Well?"

"No," I said.

"Then seems to me there's more than just fear here. There must be a thousand legends an' stories in these mountains, an' most o' them mean somethin'. Ain't gonna dismiss 'em 'less I got good proof they ain't so."

"What do I do?" I asked.

"Cain't tell you, Wind. You'll know, I think."

I was troubled for the rest of the month by the warrior's spirit. It might have been a dream, or it might have been real. I don't know. But when it passed, I felt alive again.

The coming of summer brought us a new hunting season, and we talked of where to go.

"Perhaps the Crow will be back on the Big Horn this summer," I said. "Maybe we can hunt and fish there by their camps."

"Crow're far north o' there," Bear told me. "It must be the Snake or the Yellowstone."

"The Yellowstone then," I said. "I have bad dreams on the Snake."

"You dream o' battles an' white men there," Bear said, laughing. "You have a strong spirit for medicine. You'd be prized by the Crow."

"Their warrior spirit already wants me," I said. "I think I ought to have some peace for a while."

"Well, it's the Yellowstone, then. It's a special place, as is the Big Horn. Plenty o' game an' lots o' company."

"Company?" I asked.

"Nez Perce, Blackfoot, Flathead, Sioux. Then there's soldiers an' trappers. It's got to be almost civilization."

I laughed at him.

"You'd rather go somewhere else?" I laughed.

"No," he said. "It's a place that speaks to my spirit."

We talked some about the Yellowstone. When we darkened the cabin and went to bed, a strange silence hung in the air.

"Wind, you ever miss Ohio?" he asked me.

"Why would I? I have a home here on this mountain. I belong here," I said, pausing. "I belong here with you."

"Yer growin' up," he said. "You've got more'n two hairs on yer chin. It must be more'n a boy's wish to have fun that binds you here. It must be a man's wish to have a life here."

"I think it is," I said. "I've marked each winter that's passed here. I'm fifteen years old. That's not a man in Ohio years, but it's a man in Teton years."

"Yes," Bear sighed. "I brought you somethin' from the rendezvous, you know."

"All this time you've hidden it?" I asked.

"Yes," he said, lighting the lamp. "I wanted to surprise you. When yer spirit was troubled, it wasn't the time."

"What is it?" I asked, jumping to my feet.

"Here," Bear said, taking a box from behind the woodpile.

I tore it open and pulled out a treasure.

"Books!" I yelled. "They're wonderful."

"Little Frenchy gal found 'em fer me. Thought you might like to read some."

"They're wonderful," I told him.

I opened the first up and froze in silence. The words were foreign to me. Then I realized what it was. I picked up another and another. They were all in French.

"Bear," I said, a smile coming to my lips, "they're all in French."

"Yeah?" he said. "Looks all the same to me."

"Bear," I said. "You don't understand. I can't read them. I don't know how to read French words."

"Oh." He frowned.

"Don't be sad," I said, laughing. "Don't you see how funny it is? You know French, but can't read. I can read, but don't know French."

We looked at each other for a few minutes. Then we burst out laughing. We laughed our way well into the night. Then we put out the lamp and fell into a sound sleep.

XV

The Yellowstone River flows from its source in the Rocky Mountains through the heart of Montana into the Missouri River. During my years with Bear, we'd hunted and fished nearly every mile of the river. But the upper Yellowstone Valley, where the river winds through canyons and cascades hundreds of feet over waterfalls, is the most magnificent place I've ever seen.

The first year I rode along the river, we saw only bears and deer. Sometimes I'd spot a small party of Indians, but white men were strangers, and the Indians were busy. They paid little attention to us.

This year the river was still full of game, but now there was no scarcity of white men. Some were gold hunters. Others were trappers and adventurers. We saw no mountain men like ourselves, and Bear told me none would come again to the Upper Yellowstone. Mountain men didn't trust company, and there was too much of it on the river.

We passed on by most of the men, ignoring them as was our way. I saw they stared at us as if we came from another world. Perhaps we did.

There was a new trading post north of the river, and Bear took me by there.

"Next year we'll come up here instead o' goin' to the rendezvous," he told me. "It'll be closer, and we'll likely get better goods and more news."

I watched Bear's eyes these days. There was a change in them. They were sad eyes, and I asked him if something was wrong.

"No, Wind," he said. "Jest life. I guess it was bound to happen, but looks like yer gonna have to go deeper an' deeper into the mountains to get away from people."

"Are people so bad?" I asked.

"Depends," Bear said, looking into my eyes. "Wind, people's no better or worse than anything else. Jest like that wolf. She's not bad o' herself. She hunted 'cause it was her way."

"How are people like that?"

"Some're like the wolves and the hawks. They hunt an' kill anything they can. They do it fer food, sure, but you wouldn't want to get in their way."

"People don't eat people," I laughed.

"They do, Wind," Bear told me. "They don't do it with their teeth, but they do it jest the same. They trample 'em on their way to what they think's important."

"Not all of them," I said.

"No," Bear acknowledged, smiling. "Some's like yer mother. She was a great person. Crow mighta called her Raven. Raven's a wise ol' bird. She'll take what's left by others, and make it her life. But you tangle with her, you'll find somethin'.

"Then there's people like that old elk," Bear went on.

"They's the best. They fight fer what they think, an' die 'fore they give up."

"You're like that," I said.

"No, Wind," Bear said. "I's a loner. I's a bear. I go my own way. I hole up in winter. I try to let the rest o' the world go on without me."

"Does it work?" I asked him.

"Fer me," he said. "Each man has to make his own life, though. You'll have to make yer own, too."

"I'll be a bear, too," I said.

"When the time comes, you'll go yer own way. You got time to make up yer mind."

I saw it was one of those things I wasn't to question. When he said, "when the time comes," I knew it was something I'd have to grow more to know.

We found a stretch of the river that no one else was trapping, so we settled in there. We made our camp in a small clearing, then set out to place our traps.

It was good trapping country, and we collected some fine pelts. The beavers were heavy, and we added some fox and raccoon. I swam daily in the river, but my heart was heavy. There was a feeling I couldn't put my hands on that told me something was going on. Then I woke up screaming one night.

"Wind, wake yerself up," Bear told me. "Get hold o' yerself. It's goin' to be all right."

I shook myself awake, shivering with cold.

"Wind, yer sweatin'," Bear told me, feeling my forehead. "Yer freezin' yerself."

"I had a dream, Bear," I told him.

"Is that warrior spirit after you again?"

"It wasn't that dream. It was the other."

"The Cheyenne an' the wagon?" Bear asked.

"No," I said. "It was the battle. Squirrel's death."

"Tell me 'bout it," he said.

"It was clearer this time," I said. "And there was no fire like last time."

"What'd you see?"

"I saw a white man with long blond hair. He was like someone I've seen before, but I'm not sure who he is."

"What was he doin'? Killin' the Cheyenne boy?"

"He was dying," I said. "He was clutching the grass in his right hand. His head was full of blood, and he was dying."

"An' Squirrel?"

"He was dying, too. He got shot by a soldier. I watched him die."

"What scared you, Wind?" Bear asked.

"I saw where it was. It was the Big Horn Valley. The Sioux and Cheyenne were camped all along the river."

"Was it winter or summer?" Bear asked.

"Summer," I said. "They were sweating. The Sioux were bare chested."

"Did you see who won the battle?" Bear asked.

"The soldier with the blond hair was about the last of the white men. He died. The Sioux wiped them out."

"We'd best be careful. If the Sioux've taken on the army, they won't hang around the Big Horn. They'll head west or north."

"It was the gathering Squirrel talked about, wasn't it?" I asked.

"Yes." Bear frowned. "It'll be the end o' the Sioux. Th'army'll never put up with a massacre. They'll wipe out the Sioux."

I sat and looked at the wrinkles in Bear's forehead. There were more of them than I'd seen before, and I wanted to reach out to him. But his eyes told me that he was elsewhere.

The next morning, I splashed my way into the river. The cool water washed away some of the terror I'd felt since the night before, and I laughed out loud. I dove under the water and chased a trout. It was one of my favorite games, and it took my mind off the dream.

I'd never worried about my dreams before, but this one changed all that. Bear told me the Indians believed that fire in a dream meant a warning. Without it, the dream had already happened.

I didn't understand why I should have a dream like that. Why was it important for me to know there was a battle on the Big Horn? But one thing seemed to come across to me that was stranger than the rest. I was certain there had been a battle and that Squirrel was dead, yet there was no proof.

When my head broke out of the water, a shot rang out through the valley. There was a splash in the river behind my head, and I looked in the direction of the shot.

It was a foolish thing to do. It only gave the shooter a second chance. But the surprise possessed me, and I stood frozen, looking at my would-be killer.

He was a soldier on horseback, not a whole lot older than me. As my eyes looked up at him, his sergeant slapped the rifle from his hands. He yelled something at him, and I stood up in the river.

"I am no enemy," I shouted to them. "I am called Wind. I trap the river. I am brother to the Crow, who scout for the army."

"Come out o' there slow, boy," the sergeant called to me. "Keep yer hands where we can see 'em."

"I hold no weapons," I said. "But I am naked. If you would bring my clothes to me, I would be a better host to you."

"It's a trick, Woods," the man who'd shot at me yelled. "These Sioux're tricky. They even speak English."

"Randolph, you're a fool," screamed the sergeant. "You ever seen a Sioux with blond hair? Go get his clothes."

The man splashed his way through the river and picked up my clothes. He left my rifle and my pistol on the ground. Then he rode past me and threw the clothes in my face.

"You are welcome in our camp, Sergeant," I told him. "Will you not come and share our food with us?"

"Who is with you?" asked the sergeant.

"A wild man who don't take to fool questions," boomed out Bear's voice from behind them.

I saw he had them covered with his rifle, so I raced out of the water and slipped my clothes on. Then I returned with my rifle in hand to the river.

"I'd appreciate it, boy, if you'd tell that wild man to lower his rifle," the sergeant said. "We come in peace."

"You call it peace to shoot boys swimmin' in the river?" Bear yelled. "Maybe you'd like a shot past yer ear?"

"It's all right," I told Bear. "The sergeant took care of that. I've invited them to our camp."

"Then you may go on yer way or come to share our food," Bear said. "Wind has opened his heart to you."

The soldiers looked at their sergeant, and he signaled them toward our camp. Bear mounted his horse and fol-

lowed them. I passed out cornmeal cakes and dried venison to everyone and took a seat.

"You got to excuse my men," the sergeant told me.
"We been huntin' down hostiles since July. General
Terry's got most o' them Sioux corraled, but some o'
them's headed west."

"There was a battle on the Big Horn," I said.

"Heard about that, did you?" the sergeant asked.

"No," I said. "I saw it in a dream. Many soldiers died
there."

"Most o' the Seventh Cavalry. They got General
Custer, too."

"Custer," I mumbled, an image of the blond man racing past my eyes. "Now I remember, Bear," I said. "The
man I saw die was Custer. I met him at Ft. Riley in Kan-
sas. He was kind to me, and told me of the war."

"Hey, this kid's crazy," one of the soldiers said. "He
didn't dream this stuff. He must've been ridin' with the
Sioux."

"Yeah, Sarge," another said. "Dreams don't tell about
no battles."

"Quiet," the sergeant commanded. "I seen it before.
Never with a white man, though. You part injun?" he
asked me.

"No," I said. "I can't explain it. I've never had a dream
like that before."

"Well," said the sergeant. "It's ever bit true. Old
Custer charged the whole injun camp with a few com-
panies o' cavalry. They got themselves scalped an' cut up
bad."

"Them men had things done to 'em wasn't decent,"
said one of the soldiers.

"I know," I said, swallowing hard. "I watched the Cheyenne torture a friend of mine. It was a long time ago, but I still remember."

"You watched?" asked a soldier. "What kind of . . ."

"Quiet, you!" Bear yelled. "Wind wasn't no taller than a tree stump. He was trapped by a wagon. Cheyenne did it so he'd have to watch. That's torture, too."

The man turned his eyes away from me.

"How'd you come to be here, boy?" asked the sergeant.

"I was goin' West with some people. My folks are dead. The Cheyenne ambushed us, and I was taken captive. They might have killed me, but Bear bought me."

"Bought you?" asked a soldier. "You mean that man owns you?"

"Wind is owned by no man," Bear shouted. "He's as free as a cloud."

"So you say," the sergeant said. "I've seen such things before. Boy, if you want to leave, you may come with us."

"When Bear says that I am free, he is right," I told them. "This man has saved my life a hundred times, and he has taught me about life. He has been a father to me. I don't wish to leave him."

"Yer not afraid to go?" the sergeant asked.

Bear laughed.

"When Wind was nine, he shot his first bear," Bear told them. "He's killed buffalo, elk, cougar, and even a she-wolf. He's walked the mountains fer six winters, and he's seen more Indians than you'll ever see. Afraid?"

Bear laughed again.

"Can we do anything fer you at all?" the sergeant asked.

"You could post a letter for me," I told him.

"Gladly," the sergeant answered.

I went into my knapsack and pulled out some paper. I wrote a short note to Martha and a longer one to Helen. I put them into two yellow envelopes Maurice had brought me years ago and wrote on them the names and towns they were to go to.

"If you are asked where I am, tell them only that I am well and happy," I said, handing the letters to the sergeant. "I have found my place, and it has found me."

"You men watch out fer the Sioux," a private yelled.

Then they got on their horses.

"We'll git them Sioux," said one of them. "Old Terry rode most o' them into the dust. I heard one trooper killed three squaws and four or five little bucks himself."

"What of the men?" I asked.

"To kill them Sioux, you got to kill 'em all," the soldier added. "Them bucks'll ride away an' leave their women an' kids. If we left 'em alone, they'd stay away fer good. After we clean out a village, the bucks fight."

"But to kill children," I said.

"They grow," the soldier said, smiling out of the corner of his mouth. "Little bucks git to be big bucks."

"Come, Wind," Bear told me. "We will talk o' this later."

When night came, I turned to Bear.

"I can't rejoice to hear that soldiers are killing children," I said.

"Yer o' the mountains, Wind," Bear told me. "You cain't understand them prairie people. They only know Indians as raiders an' killers. Red men kill white kids an' white women, so soldiers kill red women an' red kids."

"Don't tell me of death," I shouted. "I watched my

friend Jerome be cut apart piece by piece. But I would not kill a child to make up for it. Children are children. They are not warriors."

"I would not kill no woman either," sighed Bear. "I have lost a woman an' a son to the Sioux, but I'd not bring such sorrow to a man."

"Well, one thing good has come of this," I said. "We can camp along the Big Horn again next summer."

"No," Bear sighed. "I don't think I'd ever want to do that now."

"I understand," I said.

"Ain't 'cause o' the battle, Wind," he told me. "It's th'end o' the West. The Sioux for all their ways were the last o' the great tribes. The day o' the Indian is over. Our day may be, too."

I thought of that as I slept that night. My dreams were not disturbed. They were filled with cool rivers and beaver pelts. Snow and sunny days. I didn't know pain or trouble that night. They would have to leave me alone for a while.

XVI

The soldiers were not the only visitors to our camp on the Yellowstone. All sorts of men would come and go along the river, stopping to visit and exchange the latest news. These guests were always welcomed by me, but Bear was more of the mountain than I was, and he kept a suspicious eye open.

Just as fall was settling in and we were preparing to break camp and return to the mountains, five men rode up to our camp and dismounted.

"Good afternoon, friends," a tall man with an ugly, unshaven face said. "I wonder if we could trouble you for a cup of coffee."

"You are welcome in our camp," I said, smiling to them. "I am called Wind, and this is Bear," I said, pointing to him.

"Pleased to know you," the tall man answered.

"We've not much in the way of food, but you're welcome to share some dried buffalo meat," I told them.

"That'd be right fine," the man told me. "You men trappin' the river?"

"We jest do a little trappin' fer the sport," Bear said to

them. "We jest get by as best we can. You know how it is, trap a little, hunt a little."

"We're much the same ourselves," a big burly man with a mustache said.

"Bear," I said, my eyebrows raised, "we trap more than a little. Why this is the best beaver year we've ever had."

I saw a word of warning in his eyes, but I didn't understand why he should tell these men something that wasn't true.

"I'd surely like to see them beaver pelts," said a third man. "I'm right partial to beaver."

"Let me get one of them." I smiled, scrambling off.

I returned with a pelt and handed it to the tall man.

"This is purely nice work, boy," the man said. "You do this yourself?"

"Me and Bear," I said.

"Right nice work," the burly man said, fingering the pelt.

Bear remained silent, taking a rag and polishing the barrel of his rifle. His look was none too friendly, and the strangers grew nervous.

I wanted to tell him to put the gun away, but it was not my place to tell him what to do. So I went on with my visit, and he went on polishing his rifle.

"You have a lot of traps hereabouts?" asked one man.

"Sure. All around here. But we're pulling them out pretty soon," I told them.

"Just two of you? All those pelts and just the two of you?" asked the tall man.

"We're enough," I said.

"Say, Bear," said the burly man. "That's a mighty fierce rifle you got there. Mind if I take a look at her?"

Bear turned the gun around and stuck the barrel in the burly man's face.

"You see well enough, or maybe I should bring her a bit closer?" Bear asked him.

The burly man stood up and stepped back.

"I believe we might be strainin' our welcome," he said.

"Not at all," I said. "You haven't finished your coffee."

"I believe we'll be headin' on, boy," the tall man told me, getting up, too.

"You wouldn't want to forget and leave with that pelt, would you?" asked Bear, noticing one of them carrying it away.

"Why, Walter, I's ashamed o' you," said the burly man. "We apologize for Walter, friend. He just ain't too smart in the head."

"Have a good journey," I told them. "Where'd you say you were headed?"

"Oh, we'll be around," said the tall man, flashing a tough look at Bear. "We'll be around."

When they rode off, I turned to Bear.

"How come you were mean to them?" I asked. "Why'd you point that gun at them?"

"Wind," said Bear. "You shouldn't've said all that to them boys. Now we got to kill 'em."

"Kill them? Why would we have to kill them?"

"They's a type I seen before. They robs trappers. If they worked honest, I'd given 'em pelts. But they aims to take what ain't theirs."

"They were going to rob us?"

"Why'd you think he wanted my gun? If he'd got it, they woulda robbed us right then. Probably shot us, too."

I froze for a minute or two. I reflected on their words.

Yes, they asked more about the furs than about us or what we'd seen. That wasn't natural.

"I'm sorry, Bear," I told him. "I set us up real nice. Now they'll come after the furs for sure. I even had to go and show them off."

"Not yer fault, Wind," he told me. "It's what I like 'bout you. Yer simple. Whole world's good in yer eyes. Wish I could be like that again."

"What do we do now?" I asked.

"Pack up fast as we can. We'll get goin'. I'll show you the rest tonight."

We packed the mules and saddled our horses. When everything was ready, we rode off down the river. When night came, Bear made our beds in plain sight beside the river.

"Shouldn't we camp in a cave or something?" I asked. "We can't defend this spot."

"Don't aim to," Bear explained. "If we fight those wolves in daylight, one o' us or both likely'd get killed. This way we can pick our time. They'll come to us."

"But we'll be sitting ducks in the moonlight. They can shoot us from the river."

"If we was in our beds, they could. But we'll put some brush in our blankets, then hide an' wait. They'll think they got us. We might be able to git one or two o' them 'fore they figure out what's comin' off."

"I get the idea," I said. "There's only one thing."

"Ain't goin' to be easy. You never shot at a man, right?"

"That's what I was going to say."

"Don't think o' these as men. Think o' them as animals. They's worse than wolves. Wolves don't hunt their own kind."

We waited, lying under the trees. I had my rifle ready and my pistol in my belt. We waited for hours, my eyes growing heavy with slumber. At last, though, I heard horses splashing in the river. Then there was a wild yell, and the air exploded with shot.

I looked in horror as my bed blew apart. At least five bullets tore what would have been me to pieces. I turned my rifle at the tall man, and Bear fired at the same time.

A skinny man in cavalry britches screamed and clutched his head. Bear had shot the man dead. I aimed dead center on the tall man, and I saw him clutch his belly. Then he rolled off his horse, and tears clouded my eyes.

"They're in the brush!" the burly man shouted. "Get 'em."

I saw them charge, and I fired my Colt at the nearest one. I hit him twice, and his eyes froze in a death stare. His horse carried him right at me, and I jumped to get out of the way. His body tumbled off to the side.

"There's one o' them," yelled out a voice.

I heard the crack of rifle fire, and my leg blew up. I fell as if I'd been hit by a boulder. My head flamed with pain.

Then there was a horrible cry and the sound of the buffalo gun. I looked out of the corner of my eye just in time to see the burly man blown to pieces. One minute he was there. The next, he wasn't.

The last man tried to swing his gun toward Bear, but the man was slow, and Bear clubbed him with the buffalo gun. Then Bear took out his knife and put an end to the man.

I tried to sit up and see him, but the pain was too great.

I rolled on my side and saw a man on the right. He was dead. But in front of me, I heard a groan.

"No, don't," I heard the tall man's voice say. "I meant the boy no harm. It was all Howard's idea to rob you. Ask the boy. He's still alive. I saw him."

"Wind," Bear called to me, "do you live?"

"I'm here, Bear," I cried to him. "It's my leg. It's blown up."

"Come with me," Bear ordered the tall man, dragging him before me.

"Tell the man I didn't shoot you, boy," the tall man pleaded. "Tell him to let me be."

"I saw you," I mumbled through the pain. "You led them. You shot our beds. You would have murdered us in our sleep."

"That was Howard and Walter," he sobbed. "I couldn't shoot a boy in his sleep."

"You did," I said. "I saw you. Now you stand there with my bullet in you and ask your life."

"There's kindness in you, boy," the tall man said. "I saw your eyes. They's gentle eyes. I'd not have my death trouble 'em."

"I'll kill him fer you, Wind," Bear said. "Any manner you choose. Cheyenne fashion, if you'd like."

"No, please," begged the tall man. "Don't cut me up. I don't want to die."

"Do it as you choose, Bear," I said. "I'm burning up with pain. Do it as you please, but do it."

"You'll suffer for that, boy," the tall man said. "The devil will take you for this."

"God would not let you live, animal," I snarled at him.

"You are the worst kind of man. I'd not let you live so that you could kill someone else."

Bear led him away, and I heard nothing more of him. I noticed Bear's knife was bloody when he came back, but I didn't ask him how he'd done it.

"Why did I have him killed, Bear?" I asked. "He was right about the devil. It was wrong."

"It was justice, Wind," Bear answered. "There's only the law o' the mountain out here. It never brings a smile to kill a man, but we must trim the bad, jest as a scar must heal."

"Will I heal?" I asked. "My leg feels as if it isn't there."

"Come, Wind," Bear said. "I will see to it."

He tied a strip of his shirt around my thigh, twisting it until the bleeding stopped. Then he took me in his strong arms and carried me to the river.

"I'm dying, Bear," I said to him. "I don't want to die," I cried, clutching him with terror.

"You ain't goin' to die, Wind," Bear said. "Not if I've anything to say 'bout it."

He carried me to the river and set me down into it. The cool rushing of the water soothed the fire inside me, and Bear gently undressed me. I saw my trousers were shredded by the bullet. I had my Shoshoni shirt on, and I bid him take care of it.

"I will, little Wind," Bear told me. "You'll live to wear it again."

"Will I?" I asked.

"Yes, and as a man," Bear said. "Indians believe a boy becomes a man when he kills his first man."

"I'm not really a man, you know," I said. "Just a boy trying to be one."

"You are a man, Wind," Bear told me, stroking my feverish head with a wet rag. "You walk bravely. You need not fear death."

"What is death?" I asked, feeling my strength failing me.

"An end," Bear said. "A simple thing, really. Our spirit can then be at peace, not bothered by others."

"I don't want to die," I said, clutching him with what strength remained to me.

"There's too much life in you fer such talk," Bear said.

"I feel it, Bear," I said. "I feel the life leaving me. I can't feel my legs or my arms. All I know is what's in my eyes."

"It's the river, Wind," he told me. "It takes away the pain."

"It won't take away the bullet, though."

"That I must do," Bear said. "It will bring great pain to you, but it must be done."

"When?" I asked.

"Now," he told me.

He left me lying in the river, my head propped on the bank. I saw my torn and twisted leg. I remembered how well it had borne me across the mountain. I wondered if I would ever run so fast again.

Bear built a fire and put water on to boil. Before long, the fire was a blazing inferno of hot coals. He boiled the small fish knife he carried. Then he put some cloths in the water. Finally, he brought out his jug and came to me.

"Wind, seems a loss to me that you should get drunk the first time to have me cut on you. The first good drunk should be at a rendezvous, with a bright-eyed French gal at yer side. But things're as they are."

I took a deep sip on the jug and felt the liquid choke off the air from my head. I wanted to throw up, but Bear held my head back. He poured more of it into me, and my head began to spin. The taste grew sweet, and my eyes began to see strange things.

The whiskey clouded my thoughts. I remember distinctly two things about that time. One was a grinding sound next to the bone in my thigh. The other was the sight of Bear brushing back my hair from my eyes, then bending his knee to pray.

I'd never seen Bear pray on his knees before. He usually did his praying on his horse or standing tall against the mountain. It was strange to think of him so small. But I guess it was why he did it, to make himself smaller in the eyes of God.

We spent too much of the fall on the Yellowstone because my leg wouldn't travel. It was slow and brittle. Bear had cut deep and close to the bone, but he'd not cut the muscle or the tendons. By the time the first snows fell, I was walking with the aid of a crutch.

We watched the heavy snows from the cabin, a great feeling of closeness in our hearts. I got out *Oliver Twist, The Last of the Mohicans,* and even *The Travels of Young George Washington* to read to Bear. He still didn't care much for Mr. Cooper, but he agreed with me that Uncas was a brave man.

XVII

Walking alone through the snow one morning, it dawned on me that I must be sixteen years old. Sixteen was almost a man, even in Ohio. I knew of boys of that age who had ridden off to fight with Mr. Lincoln's army. Joseph had taken a wife when he was seventeen. There was something strangely frightening about being a man.

Always before, I'd longed to be grown. I'd dreamed of the day when Bear and I would ride the valley side by side as men. Now that day was upon me. It wasn't what I expected. I realized that Bear had always taken me as his equal. And now that I was nearly a man, I began to fear he would no longer want me around.

There was something else gnawing on me. It was that strange thing called responsibility. I feared I owed it to my family to see them. I knew with a strange certainty that if I ever rode out of the Tetons, I'd never find my way back.

I studied the reflection of my face in a stream. There was no boyishness left to it. True, only a shadow of beard had appeared, but the lines of my cheeks were hard and firm, and my eyes burned with a fire born of knowledge and hardship.

I stood almost to Bear's chin now, and only my shoulders failed to broaden. I still had a frail look to me, as if my body refused to give up that part of its boyhood. But my voice cracked when I got excited, and there was no question I was no more a boy.

I found myself walking alone more and more, especially in the mornings. Those were times of searching, not for game or adventure as I once had, but inside myself. I searched to discover what I really was and where I really belonged.

One day while I was sitting on the mountainside, I heard the sound of a horse behind me. I turned my head slightly, so as not to startle my visitor. I caught sight of a rider, but he was too thin to have been Bear. I fingered my Colt and drew it into my hand. With caution, I stood and turned.

Before me stood a tall Sioux warrior. He was thin and tired, but his eyes flashed hatred in my direction, and he raised his war lance. With a hideous cry, he charged at me.

I rested the revolver on my left arm and took aim on his head. There was no panic in my movements, for I had killed before now, and it held no mystery for me. There was a single dread of taking life in me, but I knew here was a moment of living or dying for me.

I started to pull the trigger, but the Sioux fell from his horse. The beast charged by me, brushing my shoulder. I looked around to see if anyone else was there.

"Bear?" I called out. "Are you there?"

There was no answer, and the birds did not stir.

"Is there a friend in the woods?" I called.

Still there was no answer.

"Has a spirit killed you, Sioux?" I asked, walking toward him.

When I neared, I saw that he had not been struck by an arrow, as I had supposed. I'd heard no gunshot, so perhaps a spirit had struck the Indian. I took my toe and ran it along his side. There was the warmth of life in the body, but there was no movement. Finally, I kicked him over onto his back.

A low moan greeted my ears, and I saw where the trouble was. There were two wounds, one in the thigh and the other in his shoulder. They were bullet wounds to be sure, and I knew he'd not had the strength to strike me down. I found his horse and stretched his near lifeless body across the animal. Then I led the horse and its burden to the cabin.

"Bear," I called when we arrived. "I have a guest for you. He is in the hour of his death."

The door to the cabin opened, and Bear stuck his bearded face into the light.

"What you got there, Wind?" he asked.

"He's Sioux," I said. "Been shot."

"Wind, yer a crazy boy, but you've the heart o' the mountain," Bear told me.

We got him off his horse and dragged him into the cabin. His blood stained my fingers, and I saw he was nearly starved. There was no color in his face, and the wounds were badly festered. Bear and I started in on him immediately.

There was much to be done. His clothes were stiff with ice and had to be cut away. I set a kettle of water on the fire. When the water boiled, we filled a pot and began the scrubbing.

"Lucky it was cold, or he'd be dead," Bear said. "The cold keeps out th'evil odors. They'd killed him fer sure."

"Has he come all the way from the Big Horn?" I asked.

"Or from the Platte," Bear told me. "He's come to the land o' his cousin, the Teton Sioux. He's o' the eastern tribe."

"Why would he come so far?" I asked.

"Only he can answer, Wind," Bear replied. "Only he."

We washed his wounds and warmed his frozen body. Then Bear drew me aside and looked into my eyes.

"He's two bullets in his tough Sioux hide," Bear said. "We must git them out. You got to hold him still. I got to cut."

"I will do it," I said.

"You ain't goin' to get sick on me?"

"No, Bear. I'm a man."

Bear smiled at me and laughed.

"You'll do," he said at last.

It was the hardest work I'd ever done. The Sioux came around immediately, and I suppose he reacted the same way I would have. Two people bending over you with knives, cutting on you, is not something that you will take with a lot of calm.

His eyes grew wide, and he struggled to get up.

"Hold him, Wind," Bear told me.

There wasn't a chance in the world of me holding him still at that point, so I grabbed a metal spoon and banged him over the head. He passed out, and we went on with our work.

Bear had to cut deeply, and there was a lot of blood. My stomach rumbled, but I did what I was told. Bear got both of the bullets. Then he ran a knife through the fire.

When the blade turned white, he pulled the knife over to the Sioux.

"Hold him real still," Bear told me.

Then he held the hot knife close to the wound on the Sioux's thigh so that it sizzled the flesh. Bear repeated the action on the Indian's side. It burned the flesh black, but Bear explained it helped the wound to heal. He'd done it on my leg, but I'd been too drunk to know it.

I watched the Sioux all night. The man became conscious after a few hours, but his eyes were filled with terror. I didn't know much Sioux talk, so I tried Cheyenne. I made a gesture of friendship and showed him my Cheyenne bracelet.

"Where you get that?" he asked me in broken English.

"From a Cheyenne boy named Squirrel," I said. "I met him in the valley of the Snake River."

"He friend to you?" the Sioux asked in a whisper.

"I met him one day," I explained. "I don't think we were friends, really."

"Your heart speaks with truth," he said. "This boy was killed."

"I saw it," I said. "It was on the Big Horn. I saw it in a dream."

"He brave boy." The Sioux frowned. "Not many Cheyenne die on great river. Sioux and Cheyenne kill many long knife. Long knife come like rain then. Burn, kill, chase away all Sioux."

"You ran from the soldiers?" I asked. "Why here?"

"I follow Low Dog at Little Big Horn. After battle, we break up. Lodges burned by white chief. Squaws killed. Little ones run and shout. They die, too. I hear their cries in my dreams. We run from long knife, six of us. Now I alone."

"The soldiers shot you?"

"Long knife, yes. They follow. I go to fight them."

"You can't fight them all."

"I am last one. I will fight," the Sioux said, his teeth bared.

"Why?"

"It my fate. I am warrior. I must die as warrior."

"You could stay here in the mountains," I said. "We hunt and fish here. It is a good life."

"Why you say this? Why you help me? I try to kill you. If my heart not fail me, my war lance would carry your scalp."

"I'd have shot you before you threw," I said. "It is your life that was saved. I helped you because you are a man. I'd not have a man die when I could save him."

"But I your enemy," the Sioux said.

"Why?" I asked. "Because your skin is red and mine is white? That doesn't make sense. It seems to me that men with strong hearts are all born brothers."

"I never hear white man speak such words."

"It is wisdom born of pain. My father died in battle. My mother died when I was yet a child. I saw my friends killed by Cheyenne. But there is no hatred in my heart. I have found life with Bear, and I have found strength in myself."

"You have spirit dreams, too. You are child of spirits. Sioux hear of such. Boy alone on mountain given great soul by spirits."

"No." I smiled. "There's nothing to that. I am flesh as you are flesh."

I rolled up the leg of my deerskin trousers and showed him the scar on my leg.

"Is from Cheyenne?" he asked.

"No," I said, laughing, "from white men."

He looked deeply. There was a quiet about him now.

"White wolf prey on own flesh," he said. "Long knife kill off buffalo. Great peoples of mountains and buffalo valleys all gone. Killed or on reservation. Crazy Horse ride no more. Sitting Bull go North, but buffalo do not know Canada. I ride into sun's shadow."

"I heard a story once," I said. "It was told to me by a Crow. They believe there was a before people."

"Sioux have such tale."

"There was a warrior who lived after all the others. He did not die in battle, but was told to walk the earth until the sun shined no more. He was to search out courage and tell of the ways of the before people."

"This was his duty?" the Sioux asked.

"Yes," I said. "He must walk the world in silence, always alone with his thoughts. All he ever does is sing a song to great warriors, calling them to him."

"Can you sing this song?" he asked.

"Yes," I said. "I know it in Crow and in English."

"I do not talk tongue of my blood enemy the Crow," he said.

"I will sing it for you in my own tongue. It is the way I know it best."

"I raise my voice to the heavens,
Summoning the spirits of the mountains.
I stand tall on the high ground
And look to the buffalo valleys below.

I walk with tall shoulders,
For my bow has the true aim.
My father is the storm cloud,
My mother, the summer rain.
I am kindred to the moon and the sun,
And my brother is the wind.
I see and know all men,
For I have walked among them.
There are the raven and the snake,
The deer and the elk and the bear.
I have seen their hearts, all,
Yet I walk alone among the whispering pines;
For I am the last warrior."

"Is there a place where you hear this song?" he asked me.

"A great cliff," I said. "It is on the side of the mountain. You can look to the valleys below from there."

"There is much wisdom in this Crow who tells you this. And there is much courage and honor in your eyes. I would call you brother. My people call me Gray Fox."

"I am Wind," I said.

"You will take me to this place, this cliff?"

"When you are well."

"It will be soon," he said. "You have no fear of me?"

"I fear only what I do not understand," I said. "There would be no courage in taking my life."

"You understand much, Wind."

"Yes." I smiled.

Bear understood things, too. He knew there was something between us, and he left us to each other during the day. This went on for five days, with Gray Fox telling me of the battles and campaigns against the army. There was sadness in his voice.

"This is a battle the Sioux cannot win," I told him. "You should make a treaty."

"There is nothing to be done to save my people," he answered. "To surrender is to give up our hearts and our freedom. To give away the skies and the hills for a cage is not to save but to lose our life."

The sixth morning that Gray Fox was with us, I found him up before me. He was sitting in silence, singing to himself.

"I am much stronger," he told me when I went over. "Today you will show me the spirit cliff."

"You sure you're strong enough?"

"I am strong enough for what must be done."

I led the way on Sunrise, and he followed. When we neared the cliff, I left my horse tied to a pine tree and walked ahead.

"Leave your horse," I said. "Horses grow nervous there."

He dismounted and walked up beside me. I could see his side hurt, and there was blood rolling down his side.

"We'll go back to the cabin," I said. "You're bleeding."

"It must be as I say," he told me.

His eyes were fixed ahead, so I led the way. When we got to the top of the cliff, the wind stung my face. There was a strange feeling in my stomach, and I walked back away from the edge.

"It is as you said, a spirit cliff," Gray Fox told me.

I looked over and saw that he was standing perfectly still at the edge of the cliff.

"Wind, this is the place. There is a thing which must be done."

"What thing?" I asked nervously.

"You will not understand my way," he said. "It is my choice to die here on the cliff before the spirit."

"What are you talking about?" I asked.

"I will prepare myself to be taken by the spirit."

"You're going to kill yourself," I said.

"So it will look," he said. "But all is not as it seems."

"Why do you do it?" I asked. "Life is precious. You're giving up."

"I cannot surrender," he explained. "Yet I am a coward. I would not again feel the pain of hunger or the fire of a bullet in my side."

"You want to die," I said, turning my head from him.

"A brave death is desired above all things," he told me. "I fear it not."

"You will die now?"

"Yes," he said.

I watched him strip himself. Then he took out a pouch and painted his chest. There were bright earth colors which he explained pointed the way to heaven for him. He then painted his face. When he finished, he turned to me.

"I stand before the spirit as he first saw me at my birth," he told me. "I give you my knife and my lance. They are brave arms. May they bring you good fortune."

"I take them, but I bring nothing to give in turn."

"You have given me much, Wind," he said. "You have led me here to find my fate."

"I would not have brought you here if I'd known what you planned."

"Wind, know this," he said. "If our people, those as you and I, could decide things, the long knife and the war lance would be set aside. There would be a time of life for all things."

"Yes," I sighed.

"It will take courage to see what will follow," he told me. "You are young."

"Do you wish me to leave?" I asked.

"No. You will share my great moment. I would have it so. This is no small honor."

"I will bear it so," I said.

He took his clothes and pushed them off in front of him. He stood naked before the wind, his lips moving with his death chant.

The words fell on my ears, and a tear rolled across my cheek. Then, singing still, he closed his eyes and walked out into the air.

When he fell from my sight, I felt my heart die. There was a sadness on the cliff. I walked out and looked down. His body lay crushed on the rocks below. I walked away, taking his gifts with me. I mounted Sunrise, but his horse was gone. Perhaps the spirit had called the horse already.

I told Bear about it, but he told me not to worry.

"It's a good thing," Bear said. "Few men choose the moment o' their own death."

"I guess," I said.

About a week later, a party of soldiers rode up to the cabin. We went out to greet them, sharing our food with them that night.

"We're looking for a Sioux war party," a young lieutenant told me. "They were headed this way."

"One Sioux was here," I said. "He told us he was the last of his people."

"Where'd he go?" the lieutenant asked.

"To his death," I said. "He had two bullets in him, and he knew his moment had come."

"Do you know where the body is?" asked the lieutenant. "We were told to bring proof."

"What would you like?" asked Bear angrily. "Would his scalp do, or would you rather take his hide back?"

"Either would do, if you have them?" asked the lieutenant.

Bear's eyes caught fire, but I motioned the lieutenant away from him.

"I will take you to his grave tomorrow," I said. "He lies below the mountain on the rocks."

When the soldiers rode away that next day, Bear talked to me about them.

"They's from another world," Bear said, "but th'other world is comin'. I fear the Sioux's not th'only ones who's dyin'."

I knew he meant his way of life was passing, too. There were more men in the Tetons now. Fewer and fewer of them were trappers. More and more of them were farmers and soldiers. Less and less of them had red skin.

XVIII

Now that white men rode the Tetons freely, we saw more and more of them at the cabin. We'd never had anything to fear from the Indians, for they were in fear of the medicine on the mountain. They respected courage and strength. The men who came now respected nothing.

More than once we saw our traps and storehouse raided. More than once we killed men of our own skin. It brought a shadow upon our lives, and it darkened our hearts.

The last snows of winter had not fallen when a group of rugged, bearded men rode up to the cabin one morning. Bear moved more slowly than I did, so I grabbed my rifle and opened the door a crack. A large man rode out from the others and raised his hand in friendship.

I walked outside, resting the rifle lightly in my hands, ready to shoot if it became necessary.

"Howdy, folks," the man said. "We's hunters, like yerselves. We come in peace, an' only ask if there might be a chance fer some warm food an' honest company."

"Who's to say what's honest company?" I asked him. "We've hunted and fished these mountains since the beginning. We've fought wolves and bears and Indians, but they've never shown us a false heart. Now men come to us as brothers, but they steal and lie. My heart is heavy with their killing. I'd not wish to kill a white man again."

"Hope you ain't thinkin' o' me," laughed the man. "I'd kinda hate fer you to be killin' me, myself."

There was a smile to his face, even if it was a tired one. I wanted to keep up my tough look for them. I couldn't keep from returning his smile, though, and my heart opened to them.

"Come," I said. "Tie your horses and come inside. There is hot coffee, and we've some elk steaks."

"You might," boomed out Bear's deep voice from behind me, "be so good as to leave yer rifles on yer horses."

"Surely, friend," the big smiling man said, motioning to his men to do the same. "Let's go, boys."

There were five of them in all. They were big men, dressed in buffalo hides and buckskin. Bear was nervous, and I confess I was not at ease myself.

"There isn't a lot we can offer you," I told them. "We have some beans and the elk."

"Son," said one of them. "We been huntin' buffalo fer three months. We been wet an' cold an' tired all that time. Just now, somethin' hot would be 'bout like the fanciest steak in San Francisco."

"Buffalo, eh?" asked Bear. "You men supplyin' th'army?"

"No," said the large man who was their leader. "We hunt fer the bounty."

"Bounty?" I asked. "For buffalo?"

"Sure, son," the leader answered. "After the Little Big Horn, army put a bounty on buffalo hides. They'll pay fer the hides."

"What about the meat?" I asked.

"We don't bother with that," he explained. "We eat what we want an' leave the rest fer the wolves."

Bear stood up, fire in his eyes.

"How many hides you take in them three months?" Bear asked.

"Oh, how many'd you say, Jake?" the leader asked one of the men.

"Close to a hundred and fifty," Jake told us. "Some were just calves, though, an' we don't know if the colonel'll pay full fer 'em."

"Those buffalo'd feed hundreds. Yer takin' the life from hundreds o' Indians. Children'll starve fer what you've done."

"You ain't tellin' me nothin' I don't know, mister," their leader said. "Army pays a bounty on them hides 'cause it wants the buffalo killed off. They wants the critters wiped out so them injuns'll keep to the treaty. Railroad'll be at the Yellowstone in a winter or two. Then farmers'll be tillin' the prairies."

"Ain't right," Bear said. "These mountains weren't meant to be farmed. They's meant fer men to hunt an' fish. They's meant fer men who's men to be men. How's a man goin' to be a man if some farmer's plowin' up his huntin' grounds."

"They calls that progress, friend," Jake said. "There's sad times ahead fer these mountains. My daddy hunted the Yellowstone with the Sioux an' the Cheyenne. Now they's all gone."

There was no more talk that evening. Bear dished out food for everyone, but the eating was done in silence. As I searched the faces around me, I saw they all belonged

somewhere in the past. Buffalo hunters killing off their
way of life, opening the West to the farmers who would
chase off the elk and the deer. The farmers would chase
us off too, I feared.

In the days after the buffalo hunters left, I watched
something unknown and unseen gnaw on Bear. His forehead was wrinkled, and I knew troubles rested there. Finally, he led me to the side of the mountain one afternoon.

"Wind, I've a place to show you," he told me.

I followed him to a small meadow overlooking the
river.

"This place is my favorite," he said to me. "It's where
my spirit'll dwell after I'm dead."

"That's a long way off," I said, laughing.

"Maybe," he said. "Maybe not."

"What are you talking about?" I asked. "You're as
strong as ten men. If anyone dies, it's likely to be me."

"No, Wind," he said seriously. "Each winter my bones
grow colder. My heart chills with the thousand deaths
I've seen. My eyes cloud with the memories of other
times."

"That's stupid," I said. "If anyone's eyes should be
cloudy, it should be mine. I've seen the death of nearly
everyone I've loved."

"Wind, listen to me. There's a way to things in the
mountains. You got to listen while I tell you."

"I will," I said, sitting down beside him on a large rock.

"The Crow have a legend about life. They say each day
a man is born, a star appears in the sky. The life o' the
man is linked to the life o' the star. Some stars is bright
and shine forever. Others shine bright fer only a short

time, then dim the rest o' their lives. Others never burn bright. They jest blink. Others still shine brightest o' all, but fer only the shortest o' times."

"Which is best?" I asked.

"Fer me, the last. I's a man born to thunder. Wind, I was born o' violence, an' I should die o' it. I's not a man to die in his sleep with all his teeth fallen out. It's not the way it should be."

"You're not going to kill yourself?"

"No, Wind." Bear frowned. "That would be takin' the will o' the spirits into my own hands. No, my death'll come on its own."

"In a few years," I said.

"Soon," Bear said.

"No," I shouted. "I need you too much. I don't care about silly stars or spirits or mountains. I just care about you."

"Stop it, Wind," Bear growled. "Yer a man now. You got to understand this. My spirit won't be at peace unless you do."

I sat still and silent for a while. My eyes were clouded with tears that would not fall. All around me, life was shrouded with winter. It was a funeral scene, and I could not bear it. Finally, I turned to him.

"Why?" I asked.

"Wind, my star is dyin'. The West is changin'. Soon, this life will be no more. It ain't good fer a boy. You'll end up melancholy an' all alone. Believe me, Wind. I know. You'll end up like yer friend Gray Fox—fightin' against time. Time's the worst enemy o' all. You cain't beat it. It'll eat away on you till yer dead."

"It's the life you've taught me," I said. "It's the life I'd write for myself. It's my choice."

"This life is no more, Wind. Look around you. Where's the Indians? Where's the buffalo? Where's the elk an' the bear? Where's my brothers, the Crow? They's all gone. The worst curse a man can have upon him is to outlive his time. He's out o' place. He don't belong with people, an' he don't belong without 'em. He's alive, but inside he's dead, rememberin' the way things were before."

"Like the last warrior," I said. "He's searching the whole world alone, never finding the life that was before."

"Yes," Bear said. "He's all filled with sadness. I'd not write that life fer you."

"I understand," I said.

"Wind, I've had two sons. One died too young fer me to know him. Th'other was a Crow boy. He was a part o' his people—o' the rocks an' the streams an' the hills. He was never a part o' me like you is. Even if yer not o' my blood, yer o' my heart. Our hearts bein' the same, that's what counts."

"Yes, Bear."

"I got a demand to make o' you. You got to promise me that when my day comes an' my spirit leaves fer the world o' spirits, you'll leave, too. You'll take what you want from the cabin, sell the pelts an' the mules, an' head fer yer family. Go to Denver or to Oregon. But seek out them that's close to you. They can help you find yerself in that other world."

"It will be a strange land, and I'll be an intruder," I objected.

"No, Wind," he said. "You can read an' write. Yer young yet, an' you can learn the ways o' them others."

"But my star may be of the mountain," I said.

"No." He smiled. "Yer star is in the heavens. I see it in yer eyes. There is somethin' there that's timeless. It's not to be fer you to pass yer days here. One day you'll come back, I think. But you'll go on t'other things fer now. You'll raise fine children an' tell them o' the before times."

"Yes," I said, smiling. "And I'll tell them of Bear."

"Promise me," Bear said, his eyes full of fire.

"I promise," I said, swallowing a sob.

"It's a hard thing to do," he told me. "But there's rightness in it."

"Bear," I said, turning his shoulder to me, "I love you. I never knew my father, but I couldn't have asked him to have been better than you have been to me."

"Wind, my heart has a gladness in it, thinkin' o' you as a son. I would have it so always."

"It's been that way for a long time now," I said. "We have not spoken it, but it has been in our hearts."

"Yes," Bear said, "in our hearts."

"You will go back now?" I asked.

"Yes," he sighed. "I feel the clouds gathering, and there is much to do."

"I don't see any clouds," I said.

"Not those kind o' clouds," he told me. "The clouds that sing my death chant. But they must wait fer my moment."

"They will wait a long time."

"No," Bear said, pausing, "we can expect them soon."

XIX

The coming of spring greeted my eyes as always. The snows thawed, and the mountain flowers appeared to signal the renewal of life. All life had suddenly become precious to me, and in spring, I saw a new hope for me, Bear, and indeed, our world.

Winter did not take him. We hunted and fished and trapped as always, walking side by side the hills and rivers through the snow. There were dangers, but Bear's star shined brightly. No harm came to either of us.

Spring signaled a time of much work for us. We had to prepare the winter's skins and furs for our trip to the trading post on the Yellowstone. I didn't ask Bear this year if I could go along. I saw in his eyes that I would.

For days and days we brushed the beaver and fox pelts. A brilliant shine came to the furs, and we expected a good price for our wares. If the day of the mountain man was passing, the demand for his goods was not. The good ladies of New York, Boston and Philadelphia longed for the furs that we would bring.

We finally finished with the furs. I was stacking them one morning when Bear rushed into the storehouse.

"Wind, come. There is something you must see," he

told me, pulling my arm nearly out of joint in his eagerness.

I ran after him along the side of the mountain. When I reached the edge of the woods, I saw what he was talking about. In the valley below was a great herd of buffalo. There were not so many as we'd seen before the army bounties had been posted, but there was one great bull that caught my eye.

"He's a great beast, eh, Wind?" Bear asked me.

"He's like the old elk," I said. "He's king of the valley right now."

"I got to hunt him, Wind," Bear said. "It may be the last great herd o' all time. It's in our valley. We must hunt it."

"Then we will," I replied. "I'll saddle the horses, and you get the guns ready."

We ran to our duties. Bear's old horse was nervous and jumped at me. I calmed him at last and threw a blanket over his back. When he was ready, I turned to Sunrise. The pony was old now, but there was a look of adventure in his eyes. He seemed ready for anything.

I led the horses out and met Bear coming the other way.

"Wind, I got somethin' here fer you. I picked her up last year at the rendezvous. I wanted to wait till you was ready, an' I guess that's now."

He handed over a huge buffalo gun, shiny new. I stroked the long barrel with my fingers, my face bright with a smile.

"Thank you, Bear," I said. "It's a fine gun."

"It'll serve you well," he said. "It is a gun fer a man."

We mounted our horses and rode down the mountain

together. We'd hunted buffalo before, but there was something special about this time. Perhaps it was the knowledge that the buffalo were dying, that their star was fading, too. Here we were, old enemies, both in our last days.

We tied the horses to a pine tree and stalked the buffalo. We were perhaps three hundred yards away, but they grazed without paying us any attention.

"Poor creatures," I whispered to Bear. "They are so great and fierce, yet they stand there to be slaughtered like pigs. It should not be this way."

"Perhaps they know their fate," Bear said. "Perhaps they simply do not run from their deaths."

"Yes," I said. "I like that better."

We walked in silence, keeping to the edge of the woods. We were careful not to startle them as we closed in. Many a hunter had been trampled by buffalo hooves.

"A buffalo steak'd taste mighty good to me jest about now," Bear told me.

"Yes," I said. "And if you want one, you shall have it."

The herd turned toward us, and I picked out a large bull to my right. I turned the gun and lined up the sights. My thin arms held the gun steady, and I rechecked the primer. It was ready. I aimed again and fired.

The air exploded with my shot, and I fell backward from the recoil. I bounced up and saw Bear standing above me, his eyes full of laughter.

"You got a bit o' growin' still to do," he said, smiling.

I looked at the buffalo. The herd was moving away. Before us, two great bulls lay still in the snow. They were fine beasts, and I knew there would be meat for many days.

"Let's go git 'em, Wind," Bear said.

I got the horses and followed him to the buffalo. I never found joy in examining my kill, as some do. I made the throat cut to let the blood drain. Then I waited for Bear to help with the skinning. Suddenly I felt the ground shake.

"Wind!" I heard Bear call, a tremble coming to my spine.

I looked behind me and saw the huge bull we'd seen from the mountain charging me. The horses scattered, and I fumbled with the gun. I watched the bull charge, knowing there was no time to load. I turned my eyes toward the beast, preparing myself for the death that awaited me.

But it was not to be. Bear came running out, yelling and waving a blanket at the bull. The creature stopped, fixing his eyes on Bear. I hurried to load the gun. But as I raised the gun to fire, the bull charged. I took dead aim, and the air again exploded. I tumbled to the ground, landing against the side of my kill. My back hurt, my shoulder ached, my head was full of clouds. Still, I hurried to my feet to see about Bear.

Before my eyes, the great bull lay dead. There was no life left in him, but I saw no sign of Bear. I knew the beast must lay on top of him, so I threw away the gun and raced across the field.

"Bear!" I screamed in terror. "Bear!"

There was pain in my chest as I ran without breathing. My legs took me up into the air, and I felt myself racing the wind. I came to the bull, but found Bear not under, but beside the beast.

"Bear?" I asked.

"Wind, you killed the creature sure. Yer the shot I taught you to be. You killed the bull, but I fear he's killed me."

"What?" I asked.

"I heard of a legend among the Flathead. It's 'bout a man who they said couldn't be killed by a livin' creature."

"What are you talking about?" I asked.

"Them Flathead said it was me. I couldn't be killed by a livin' thing."

"That's good," I said. "Then you can't die."

"You don't understand, Wind," Bear told me. "You killed that buffalo 'fore he got me. His death was upon his eyes when he gored me."

"He gored you?" I asked. "I thought he just landed on you."

"Yer bound to see it," Bear said, his face contorted with pain. "Look."

He turned on his side, showing the gory mess that had been his back.

"I'm goin' to die, Wind," he told me. "I read it in the clouds."

"I can help you," I said. "I can fix you up. You'll see."

Before he could answer, his eyes closed. I thought for a moment that he was dead, but it was only the pain that had brought slumber.

I screamed to the horses, and they came. I heaved Bear's huge body upon my shoulders and got it across his saddle. I tied him on his horse, then leaped on Sunrise. Then I got back off.

"I promised you buffalo," I said to Bear. "You shall get your strength from the beast that near killed you."

I cut two great strips from the shanks of the beast and

leaped back on Sunrise. Then I rode briskly back to the cabin.

I tended him all night. I bathed his great body and seared the wound with a white hot knife. But the tear on the inside of him, I could do nothing for. When he came to consciousness, his eyes were heavy with death.

"I must see the sky," he said.

"There is a chill in the air," I said. "It is not good for you."

"I must see the sky," he said again. "I must see the stars and the moon and the trees. This I must do."

I opened the window and covered him with the great bearskin coat to ward off the cold.

"Read the stars fer me, Wind," he whispered.

"I can't read the stars," I said. "I don't know them."

"Read 'em with yer heart. What do you feel when you see 'em?"

"All the wonders I've seen before, and yet there's more. There's a haze upon the moon, and a warm glow among the stars."

"The moon mourns the passin' of a star," he told me. "She wears a veil o' mournin'."

"How do you know a star is dying?" I asked. "I don't see it."

"I feel it, Wind," he said. "Jest as a man cannot outlive his star, a star cannot outlive its man."

"I never thought of that," I said. "Now you will take some meat. I cut steaks from the bull that gored you. You will find strength from this."

"I cain't," Bear said. "My stomach's full o' fire. I cain't eat."

"You must try," I said.

"It's no use," Bear said. "I'm passing."

"You can't die," I said. "I need you. I won't let you die. I will have you live. My spirit is strong. I will lend you some of my strength."

"No, Wind," he said. "I'd not have it so. Look at me. I could never go to Denver or Oregon. My place's here. But my time's past. I couldn't be happy among farmers an' soldiers. I'll pass lightly with gladness in my heart."

"And what of me? I need you."

"Wind, understand this. I choose the moment o' my death. It's a death I'd have written fer myself. What kind o' death would it be fer a man o' the mountains to be back shot by a thief or knifed by a saloon gal?"

"There is so much life in me," I said. "I want to share it with you. What good is living when no one cares? What good is there in gladness that isn't shared? What good are tears if there is no one to cry for?"

"Wind, hear me," Bear said. "You've always honored me in my life. I never asked you to be a friend. I never asked fer yer love. These things you gave freely to me. You've been the best part o' my life."

"And the cause of your death."

"If it is so, then it's that much better," he said. "Life should come out o' death. If I could give you yer life, it would brighten my spirit."

"You have done it from the first day, Bear," I said. "You delivered me from the Cheyenne. You nursed me when I was sick. You taught me the ways of the mountains. You gave me courage and strength."

"Not courage," Bear said. "It's born to yer heart. It's been with you from the beginning."

"What would you have me do?"

"Honor my death as you've honored my life. It's my choice that it be now. When my eyes cloud, honor yer promise. It would weigh heavy on my mind fer you to be alone."

"I can never be alone. Your memory will always burn bright within my heart."

"No, Wind," he said. "There is a chill that lies in loneliness. You've not known it. I have. There's a cloud that hangs over yer head. Maybe it's the warrior spirit. Do not go with it. Leave it behind. There is only pain to be found on that road."

"I will do as I have said."

"Look to the sky, Wind," he yelled.

I turned and saw a great flash across the heavens. There was a star falling from the sky. Its tail lit the heavens, and the earth was like in daylight. The horses stamped the ground, and a strange peace filled the cabin. When I turned to Bear, his eyes were empty. His spirit had passed.

XX

There was no sun for two days after Bear left the world of the living. There was no joy in my heart, and I feared I would never smile again. I knew what Bear meant about loneliness now, and I knew I would leave as I'd promised.

The third day it was bright. Flowers danced brightly in the meadow he'd always loved. It was here I knew he'd want to rest. From the top of the mountain, his spirit could watch out over the valley. I feared the days ahead would be filled with sights he'd not wish to see, but I knew he'd want to know what was there.

I picked a special place and dug into the earth. I never asked him what he'd want done with his body. The Crow put their dead on racks above the earth. Some tribes burned their dead. I chose for Bear the rites of his people, or at least what I would choose myself.

I dug deep into the mountain he loved so well, knowing it would hold his body with warmth. Then I carved a simple pine cross which bore two words.

"BEAR," it said in the boldest letters my hand would print. Beneath that, I wrote, "father."

It was not true according to law. But in the way hearts are joined, it was so. I knew he would approve.

I returned to the cabin and took the lifeless flesh which had been him in my young arms. I'd dressed him in his best deerskin suit. Around his shoulders, I'd placed the huge bearskin coat. I got the body on the back of a mule, the horses growing nervous at his presence. Then I bore him to his grave.

I covered him with a Crow blanket he'd had forever and laid his guns and knives beside him. They were familiar to him, and if the Indians were right about the spirit needing such things in the life after, then he would have them.

I covered him with dirt and then placed a ring of heavy rocks around the grave. Finally, I placed the brightest of the wildflowers beneath the cross and bent down on my knee.

"God, I know You're listening. I haven't spoken much to You since I left Ohio, and I wouldn't blame You if You were a little mad about it. But I've thought of You, and I've tried to live a good life, being clean of mind and body as my mother taught me.

"I know the spirits of the valley have known Bear, this man now buried here. In peace he walked the earth. In peace may he walk the world of spirits. He never dealt a man wrong, and he gave often when others could not return his gifts.

"I know this is not Ohio talk, but he'd understand it better than Helen or Martha's words. I only know You as God, but I think You must be the same one that the Crow and the Sioux know, even if they call You by a different name.

"My mother prayed to You for my life. I now pray to You for my father's soul. He was good to me, and even if he didn't often tell me, I know he loved me very much.

He died giving his life for me. A man can give no greater gift.

"I've taken Your time enough already, and I know You have a lot of people to look out after. You've always smiled on me, even when it didn't seem like it at the time. If You have a moment left over when You finish your work, give thought to me. Help me choose the right road, for my guide has left me. Help me to find the peace that dwelled within him."

I left the meadow quietly, leaving his spirit to walk it alone. My heart was heavy, and it took me almost a week to clear the cabin of his things. I chose for myself the old knife he'd used to take the bullet from my leg. It symbolized the love he gave to me.

I took his old horse out and let it go. For a moment or two, the old beast looked in my eyes. Then he understood and raced off down the mountain.

Everything was ready for me to go to the trading post on the Yellowstone, but my legs would not move. There was something unsettled about me, and I found myself walking to the spirit cliff.

Gray Fox's bones still marked his death scene, and as I looked down on the valley, I felt something touch my shoulder. There was a warmth within me as my heart was flooded with the song.

"I raise my voice to the heavens," I yelled out across the valley, "summoning the spirits of the mountains."

There was a rush of wind across the mountain, and I heard other voices join mine.

"I stand tall on the high ground and look to the buffalo valleys below," I said, knowing that the buffalo would soon be gone.

"I walk with tall shoulders, for my bow has the true aim. My father is the storm cloud, my mother, the summer rain. I am kindred to the moon and the sun, and my brother is the wind.

"I see and know all men, for I have walked among them. There are the raven and the snake, the deer and the elk and the bear. I have seen their hearts, all, yet I walk alone among the whispering pines, for I am . . ." I said, pausing.

Silence flooded my ears. The wind stilled, and the grass in the valley below ceased to move.

"I understand the song," I said. "I know its meaning. I am an orphan in this life, and I do walk alone among the whispering pines. I do know all men, but I cannot be what I am not. I am not the last warrior."

There was a violent stirring in the clouds overhead, and I wanted to run from it. There was a new strength in my legs, though, and I stood out on the edge of the cliff. The wind tore open my shirt, and my bare chest burned in the fierce wind.

"It is not to be," I shouted. "I have the courage to fight any enemy I can see. Any enemy I can grasp in my hands. But I cannot fight the enemy you place before me. I cannot fight time, for I cannot win. I will not have my bones bleached by the summer sun."

The wind died, and I walked away from it. There was a great storm that night, but I knew I had made my peace with the warrior spirit. He would not call for me again.

I saddled Sunrise and tied the buffalo gun on his side. I carried the Colt revolver and my army rifle at my side. The mules were laden with the furs and skins, and I tied them securely each to the other. The lead mule's reins I carried in my left hand.

I rode over the mountain, pausing only briefly in the meadow by Bear's grave. I knelt beside the cross and prayed a last time there.

"God," I said, "watch over the spirit of my father, Bear. I keep my promise to him and leave in peace his spirit. Protect him from the onslaughts of time. His heart and mine are one."

I rose to my feet and mounted my horse.

"Bear, hear me," I yelled. "I came to you a boy, naked and afraid. I go from you a man, clothed with courage and experience. I go to seek my fortune, leaving you behind. I must now give back to you your ways and seek those of my own people. But you will always speak to me as 'Wind,' and I will always know your voice."

I rode down the mountain on my way to the Yellowstone. There would be gold for the furs and the mules, and I would make my way to Oregon. I wondered if Thomas and Isaac ever got to California. I'd soon find out.

There would be adventure ahead for me, and life and love. But I would never again stand tall on the high ground and shout down to the valleys. And I would never again feel my heart so close to my father of the mountains, the man who called himself Bear.

As I rode on, a tear appeared and trickled down my cheek. The soft wind of spring blew across my face and swept it away. I rode north toward the Yellowstone and the world of the white man. But I knew that I would always be partly a stranger there.